SMOOTH OPERATOR

MELLANIE SZERETO

Smooth Operator

Published by Amatoria Press
Cover art by Amatoria Press

ISBN: 978-1-942522-94-2

BOOKS BY MELLANIE SZERETO

Cowboys of Science series ~

No More Mr. Gneiss Guy

Creekside series ~

Sexy Claus

Roll With It

Already Gone

Love on the Menu series ~

Love Served Hot

Red Hot Pepper

Hot Tamale Nights (coming soon)

Love on the Menu...Extra Hot standalones ~

Just Desserts

Iced Latté

A Little Appetizer

The Main Dish

Dressing on the Side

Flavor of the Day

Love on the Menu…Steamed trilogy ~

Egging Her On

Sweetening Her Up

Reeling Her In

Love on the Menu: Steamed Boxed Set

Marry Me series ~

Mom I'd Love to Marry

Dad I'd Love to Marry

Nerd Love series ~

Comma Kaze

Nerds & Babies series ~

The Nerd Next Door

The Nerd Upstairs

The Nerd Downstairs

Nerds & Babies Boxed Set

Romancing the Phone series ~

Call Me…Maybe

Smooth Operator

Hang-Ups

Telephone Lines

Dialed Up

Mixed Messages

The Homegrown Café Book Club series ~

Makin' Bacon

The Farmer Takes a Husband

The Butcher and the Baker

When Harry Met Wally

And Baby Makes 2½

The Homegrown Café Book Club Boxed Set

The Jerk Series ~

Jerk in the Box

Jerk of All Trades

Small Town Jerk

Jerk the Ripper

Hit the Jerkpot

Hit the Road, Jerk

Two Forks Hollow Christmas short story series ~

Snowballed

Two Nights Before Christmas

Mistletoe Miscalculation

All Wrapped Up

Standalone Short Stories & Novellas ~

Behind the Mask ~ contemporary romance

Death Benefits ~ paranormal romance

Diner 49er ~ contemporary romcom

Divorce Actually ~ contemporary romcom

Frostbite ~ contemporary holiday romcom

G Marks the Spot ~ contemporary romcom

Karma-lized ~ contemporary romcom

Kiss My Sass ~ contemporary romcom

Mad About You ~ romantic suspense

Not Quite Cupid ~ contemporary romcom

With Bells On ~ contemporary romcom

You Had Me at Goodbye ~ contemporary romcom

The Sextet Anthologies ~

Volume 1: Sharing

Volume 2: Dirty Dancing

Volume 3: Occupational Hazards

Volume 4: Entanglements

Volume 5: Mistletoe & Ménage

The Sextet Presents standalones ~

Playing in the Raine: A Toy Story

Bound by Voodoo: Legends

Bewitching Desires series ~

Two if by Sea

Two Knights of Passion

Two Fated for One

Two Pirates to Treasure

Two Times the Trouble

Two Roped and Ready

Two from the Triangle

Beyond Bewitching

PROLOGUE

ROSE CHAMBERS TUGGED HER STRAPLESS PUSH-UP BRA higher, lifting her boobs another inch toward the dipping neckline of her skintight off-one-shoulder dress. It matched her iridescent fingernails and her sky-blue eyeshadow, half hidden by the chin-length fall of hair on the left side of her head. The right side sported newly trimmed razor stubble. After slicking on a fresh coat of Fuck-Me-Harder lipstick, she pursed her lips at herself in the restroom mirror. “Mwah!”

A giggle-snort came from the woman beside her. The red cape, ruffled white pinafore, and black-patent Mary Janes screamed innocent girl on her way to Granny’s house, but Sienna Monroe was far more Big Bad Wolf than Little Red Riding Hood. She held out her basket of assorted individually wrapped goodies. “Want a condom before we head back out to the party?”

“That would be a no.” Casting a stink-eye at her long-time friend, Rose squeezed the lipstick tube in next to her cell phone and zipped her sequined wristlet closed. “I don’t need another asshole in my life. I already have one. Two, actually. My anal cavity and my ex.”

"Is Todd still using the excuse that Meg turned eighteen and graduated to get out of paying back child support?" Sienna skipped toward the door.

"Yep, and he's counting on me giving up on collecting it, which is not happening." Shaking off the bitchy mood about to ruin her evening, Rose led Sexy Red Riding Wolf into the slightly less noisy hallway leading into the packed bar area. Tonight was about having fun with her friends and trying to distract herself from her empty nest.

Bodies jostled her this way and that on her way to their table near the dance floor, challenging Rose to stay upright on her six-inch platform heels. Three steps from her chair, a hand skimmed the few inches of skin between the dress that clung to her backside and the top of the black thigh-high boots covering most of her legs. She snagged the grabby fingers, pulling the accoster the last several feet to her chair.

Catwoman and Batman—the newly engaged Scarlet Brinks and Nelson Whitaker, judging by the way the pussycat was rubbing against her date—had joined Poppy Gardner in her Lucille Ball costume. They looked her way when Rose plopped into her seat and tugged the middle-aged groper onto her lap.

She barely swallowed a groan at the jerk's weight, but it made lowering her voice to the deep husky tone she used for phone sex much easier. "Want to dance, big fella?"

A cocky grin slid across his face and he nodded. "You bet. On the dance floor and a few other places. What's your name, darlin'?"

With a slow blink of her false eyelashes, she parted her cherry-red lips. "Lola."

Scarlet cleared her throat and rubbed her palm down Batman's quilted abs. "L-o-l-a."

Sienna and Poppy hummed the next several bars from

The Kinks' old-but-not-forgotten song, joined by a breathy Marilyn Monroe a third of the way through the refrain. Who knew Cerise Wethers could sing like the iconic blonde?

Nelson raised his hand to his mouth and then buried his face in his fiancée's neck, obviously trying to hide a chuckle.

Realization registered in the creep's wide eyes, and he popped up from Rose's lap with a truly horrified expression. "What the fuck, dude? You look like a hooker, not a drag queen!"

"Cross dresser, not drag queen." She puckered her lips and blew him a kiss. Rising to her temporary six-foot-two-inch self, she tucked her finger under his chin. It gave her enough time to prep her voice for more 1-900-HOT-TALK huskiness. "And the word you're looking for is sex worker, smoochikins. Hooker is so last century. Are you sure you don't want to come home with me?"

He stumbled away, the crowd closing in around him and making him disappear.

"Damn, I thought for sure this costume would scare off guys like him. I guess I should've worn a strap-on under it." She dropped back into her seat and snagged her drink. "Men are such dweebs, especially when they're shit-faced. No offense, Nelson."

Batman grinned. "None taken. I'm too nerdy and sober to be a dweeb. How have you been? Does Meg like college?"

"Keeping busy." A tiny twist of melancholy squeezed her heart, but pride in her daughter's ambitiousness quickly took its place as she shrugged at Meg's best friend's dad. "She loves it. She said Em's planning to visit this weekend."

He nodded. "It's the first break she's had since she started the electrician apprenticeship. Between that and taking classes at the community college, I'm not sure when she finds time to sleep, let alone stay in touch with her friends."

Catwoman's kitty claws traced his jaw. "She's trying to make her father proud after the big deal he made about her going to college and not being a blue-collar laborer. That, and she's Supergirl."

"You're never going to let me live that down, are you?" Nelson rolled his eyes at Scarlet, but the way he held her close announced loud and clear to the world how much he adored her.

"Get a room, you two." Cerise made gagging sounds and handed them a gift with a heart-shaped wad of curling ribbon on top. "Happy engagement."

His cheeks practically glowed bright red below his eared mask, even in the low lighting, and he dropped the present on the table like a hot potato. "Are those flying dildoes on the wrapping paper?"

Grinning like a cat who planned to do some shared tongue-grooming later, Scarlet picked up the brick-sized package—most likely a sex toy of some sort. "They sure are. Oh, look. There're nipples in the background. See?"

He shook his head. "Nope, not looking. I'm only interested in seeing yours."

Her noisy purr brought a round of laughter to the whole table.

Cerise gave another breathy giggle and leaned a little closer. "Isn't the paper cute? I got a bunch of new wedding shower and bachelorette party products yesterday. I'm renting booth space for a few bridal shows in January to drum up more business for the BOB's Pleasure Palace franchises I sold this month. By the way, Rose, I got more of that lube you like and pulled two tubes for you. Raspberry vanilla ice cream and coconut cream pie."

Aiming a fake frown at her friend while trying not to snicker, Rose set her empty highball glass on its sweaty napkin. "Thanks for sharing that with the group. Are you also going to tell them about the new vibrator I bought last week?"

Acceptance of the challenge came in the form of Cerise's blonde bombshell hair-fluff. "You mean the Wagging Tongue? Or are you talking about Conan the BOB-arian?"

Sienna snorted, spurting a fountain of liquid back into her glass of cabernet. "Conan the BOB-arian! I love it!"

Poppy gave a Lucy guffaw. "I want one of those for my birthday next month, and I'm going to rename it Dicky Ricardo."

Choking sounds came from Cerise as she set her martini on the table.

A screech of feedback made the entire group flinch before a woman's cheery voice cut through the crowd noise. "Hi, everybody! I'm Carnie Burke, the new owner of The Ringer Saloon. Welcome to the first annual Halloween Buzz event!"

A chorus of hoots, hollers, and stomps drowned out Rose's and her companions' more sedate applause.

Before the commotion died down completely, their host curtsied in her thigh-skimming Bo Peep dress at centerstage and raised the microphone to her mouth. Fake blonde ringlets bounced around her bonnet. "First off, I want to thank you for coming out to the party tonight and remind you to assign a designated driver or let one of the bartenders know if you're going to need a ride home. The Ringer wants everyone to get home safely tonight. Now that we've gotten the public service announcement out of the way, we're ready to start the costume contest. Couples, you're up! Please make your way to the stage to check in, and good luck!"

Rose grinned at Scarlet and Nelson across the table. "Get moving, you two. Nobody's allowed to sit this one out."

Despite the dubious dip of his eyebrows, Batman followed Catwoman into the fray, their hands linked together and their chemistry sparking a twinge of jealousy in Rose's heart—or maybe her neglected woman parts. She had no delusions of grandeur about finding a partner in bed again, let alone in life—not that she begrudged Scarlet or Nelson their happiness.

Plopping her caddy of condoms next to her drink, Sienna leaned toward Cerise. "Hey, is that BOB thing for real? Because I absolutely need one."

"Yep." The blonde bombshell skimmed a finger over the screen of her cell several times and then shared a picture of the generously endowed vibrator in question. "And I can personally vouch for the claims on the packaging."

Rose bumped her friend's shoulder. "Conan the BOB-arian, when only a fictional dick will do."

"That would be pretty much all the time." The twice-widowed version of Marilyn scowled. "An obnoxious thirty-something jackass came in the shop today to buy some bachelor party supplies and thought he was God's gift to women. Not only did he paw my ass as I was showing him the party favors, he pretended to accidently brush his arm against my boob. Then he called me a bleach-blonde bitch when I informed him of the security cameras and suggested he get the hell out of my store before I filed sexual harassment charges. I told him I may be a bitch, but I've never dyed my hair in my entire life, and then he agreed to leave. Of course, I had a spiked collar poised to stab him in the nuts at the time."

"Out-of-towner?" Appalled on behalf of her friend, Rose wrinkled her nose. "I doubt any of the men in Bell are brave enough to risk pissing you off. You should add your pharmacology degrees and dead husbands' names to the proprietor section on the door. If that doesn't scare them into behaving themselves, nothing will."

Sienna raised an eyebrow. "I'm guessing a spiked anything to the nuts is a very effective deterrent. Men tend to be more protective of their balls than their brains."

Poppy nodded. "True. A guy I used to clean house for had at least eight athletic cups but only one football helmet."

Rose's friend's comment sparked another unwanted reminder of her ex. "Sounds like someone I know."

Her purse vibrated against her leg, hinting at a call or text, and she barely resisted the urge to see if one of her kids needed her. It was probably a telemarketer wanting to sell her a timeshare she didn't want and couldn't afford.

Bo Peep's voice rang through the bar again. "All right, folks! We're ready to get started. First, I'm going to introduce all of our contestants while you hold your reaction. Then each couple will step forward. Clap, hoot, and holler for your favorite to help decide the winners. The entrants with the loudest cheering will win bragging rights, a large pizza and soft drinks, and two free games of pool. Here we go! In the couples category, we have peanut butter and jelly, Batman and Catwoman, rum and Coke, dollars and cents, Spock and Uhura, and a pair of mittens."

A second and third round of buzzing distracted Rose from the rest of the pre-voting announcements, and she slipped her cell from her wristlet in time for the screen to light up with a fourth text.

Her son's name and his last brief message brought a surge of panic. *"Call me! ASAP!"*

She leaned closer to Cerise. "I need to head outside for a minute to make a phone call."

Not waiting for an acknowledgment, she stood and made her way through the nearly shoulder-to-shoulder mass toward the exit. Thankfully, no one slowed her with their wandering hands this time.

The bouncer pushed open the door at her approach, and the sudden racket behind her cut off mid roar as she stepped past him into the full parking lot.

After a tap on Beau's contact, she lifted the phone to her ear.

He picked up before the first ring finished. "I'm okay and Meg's okay. Dad, not so much."

Fuck. What did the idiot do now? The uncharitable thought came unbidden, like the instantaneous relief coursing through her gut, but she swallowed the bitterness. Without her loser of an ex-husband, she wouldn't have her kids. She did her best to inject some compassion into her voice, not that Todd deserved it. "Is it serious?"

"He's at Akron General. I don't know what happened, other than he cut his leg and lost a lot of blood. They've started a transfusion, but—"

"The supply is low. As usual." Her insides twisted in a knot, caught between knowing what she wanted to do and what she should do. *Well, shit. Damn my O-negative blood, and damn Todd for being the father of my children.* "I'll be there as quick as I can."

She dug her keys from her tiny purse and hurried toward her pickup several rows from the front door of The Ringer Saloon as fast as her sky-high boots let her.

Halfway across the parking lot, the groper stumbled out from between two monstrous SUVs. He swiped his sleeve across his mouth and narrowed his eyes at her. "I'm gonna kick yer pussy ass."

I don't have time for your drunken threats. She weaved through the cars leading away from him, but he followed her progress and cut her off five spots from her truck. "I'm not fighting somebody who can't even stand on his own two feet."

Headlights flashed in and out of the row a moment before a police cruiser stopped almost beside her. The driver's window eased downward, revealing a uniformed officer who looked barely old enough to shave and vaguely familiar. Had he graduated with Beau? "Everything okay, ma'am?"

She stepped closer, hoping the youngster didn't make the same assumption the drunk-and-disorderly dude had, not that she'd propositioned anyone for money. "No, actually. A close family member was in a serious accident, and I need to get to Akron General ASAP."

Despite her little white lie, the deputy gestured toward the passenger side. "Climb in. I'll be glad to take you. Just give me a second to radio in."

Keeping one eye on the loser who was still too wasted to walk straight, she rounded the car and accepted the officer's invitation by folding herself into the seat. "Thank you. I really appreciate the lift."

With a nod and a smile, he reported to the dispatcher and then flipped on his red-and-blue lights as he headed for the exit, leaving Lola's accoster in the dust.

Who knew her ex-husband could be the lesser of two evils?

CHAPTER ONE

Barton Holloway scratched at eight days' worth of beard stubble on his neck and then flipped on his turn signal for the next driveway. The lane led toward a white farmhouse set in the middle of a stand of massive oak trees, his single headlight illuminating the leaf-strewn gravel in the quickly approaching dusk.

Rose Chambers. Owner of Bell Lumber.

She would be interviewing him for the delivery driver job at her lumberyard.

He'd once had a crush on a girl named Rose in high school—long before his pair of short-lived marriages. The image of the leggy young woman with long brown hair, brown eyes, and glasses formed in his mind. He smiled, warmed by the memory. God, he missed being fourteen and not having a care in the world, other than attracting the attention of the gorgeous troublemaker four years his senior.

Rosie Kovac. I wonder where she is now.

Hopefully, this Rose would give him the opportunity to switch from long-haul driving to local deliveries. His back would sure appreciate the change. Nearly three decades of sitting behind the wheel of a big rig had taken its toll on his forty-six-year-old body.

He shut off the purring engine of his rebuilt Harley, took off his helmet, and downed the dregs of the convenience-store coffee from his insulated mug. A shudder rippled through him at the bitter aftertaste, but he shook it off. His interview took precedence over a twelve-hour nap after more than a week on the road.

Returning the mug to its holder, he engaged the kickstand and swung his leg over the seat. His legs protested the walk to the wraparound porch and the short climb up the three steps. At least the pinched nerve in his left hip wasn't to blame. Nope, this time the culprit was the combination of roughly six thousand miles in a week, the damp fall weather, and an old football injury.

Middle age sucks.

Despite being fifteen minutes early for their Saturday evening appointment, he pulled in a chilly breath and raised his fist to knock on the side door—the one Ms. Chambers, possibly his future employer, had directed him to use in her email.

Before he made contact, a husky feminine groan carried through what looked to be a partially opened window a few feet to the left of the door. "I love the feel of your balls in my hand. Do you want me to squeeze them? How about if I eat your cock and swallow it whole? I want to suck it while Ella licks my clit."

A threesome?

A hint of interest flickered behind Barton's zipper, waking him up faster than the high-octane coffee he'd chugged. Of course, jacking off to the free girl-on-girl-on-guy porn soundtrack right then and there wasn't exactly an option. Too bad his last attempt at a relationship had resulted in getting dumped about three or four years ago, because real sex would hit the spot better than going solo again.

Another reason forty-six bites.

"Yeah, just like that, baby. Mmm. Oh, that feels so good." Her sexy voice sounded closer, maybe right on the other side of the glass. She moaned again, and sucking noises joined in the fuck fest.

When he retreated a step to go wait by his bike, movement in the window caught his attention. A backlit pair of hands wrapped around a rigid dick-shaped appendage beyond the thin curtains moved up and down in a steady motion. The sucking sounds continued, along with some heavy panting and several breathy sighs, even though no mouth covered the head of the stiff cock. Was it from Ella going down on his kinky boss-to-be?

"Play with my nipples, Kip. God, I'm so close. Oh. Oh. Oh. Yes! I'm coming, Ella! Now! Oh, God! Yes!"

Keening carried to Barton's ears, and he clenched his jaw to keep from groaning with her. While he enjoyed porn as much as the next guy, voyeurism had never been on his radar. The woman had a sexy as hell voice, all low and smooth and husky, like a shot of aged whiskey gliding down his throat. Damn, he needed a cigarette, and he didn't even smoke.

No other orgasmic noises followed, which seemed a little weird, considering her steady pumping on the rod in her grip. "I hope that was as good for you as it was for me. Same time next week? Okay. Have an awesome night, Kip."

The sucking suddenly ended, and a gurgle and slurp followed.

"About fucking time you unplugged, stupid sink." The business end of a plunger appeared for a moment before she plunked it into a now-visible bucket on what was probably a counter. "I hope you enjoyed getting sucked off as much as Kip."

Barton slapped his hand over his mouth to hold in a laugh, but he only succeeded in creating a massive fart impersonation.

"Who's out there?" His no-longer-future employer whipped back the curtain and pressed her cheek against the bug screen. Her thick-framed glasses tilted, leaving them crooked across her nose and eyes, but she stared right at him. "Shit. You're here for the job interview, aren't you? You're early. I can explain, but I'm not going to. Give me a sec."

He bit down on his lower lip to keep from grinning. At least the woman owned her behavior and didn't give a damn if anyone approved or disapproved. "Take your time."

After the bang of what sounded like a cabinet closing and then faint footsteps, the door swung inward, revealing a tallish woman in baggy overalls and work boots. One strap hung down to her hip and half the bib draped across her right breast. A pert nipple poked at her flannel shirt, hinting that she might not be wearing a bra.

A perfect breast. Not too big. Not too small. Just right.

He lifted his gaze to her face as she raised the eyebrow that wasn't half hidden by a thick fall of glossy brown hair. Despite his dick swelling behind his zipper again and being caught checking her out, he offered his hand. "Ms. Chambers? Barton Holloway."

She narrowed her eyes as she met his grip with an equally firm one. Then she gestured for him to enter and led him into the room with the window—the kitchen. "Call me Rose. If you repeat any of what you overheard or speculate about it, your ass is fired. Understood?"

"Sure, but I didn't know you hired me yet." He sat in the chair she indicated, not sure whether to celebrate his new job or quit. "Maybe you should tell me more about what I'll be doing."

Leaning her hip against the counter, she crossed her arms under her attention-grabbing breasts. "Loading and unloading lumber. Standard sizes up to sixteen feet long. Plywood. Trusses. You'll be making local deliveries within twenty-five miles. Ninety percent of my customers are builders and contractors, so you'll have multiple large orders per day. Can you handle a forklift?"

He nodded and forced his eyes to stay focused on her neck and above. "Yep."

Her expression didn't change. "How about a flatbed truck? Do you know anything about repairs and maintenance on Freightliner diesel engines?"

"I can drive flatbeds, dump trucks, eighteen-wheelers, and pretty much every other kind of truck, car, and bike. Manual and automatic." He rested his elbows on the table, still studying her unreadable face. What kind of business owner hired a person and conducted the job interview after the fact? "I've done most of my own repairs on the rigs I've driven for going on twenty years. I also worked in my grandpa's repair shop before I got my CDL."

She picked up a folder from the counter, crossed to where he sat, and set the file in front of him. "That's why I'm hiring you. It's time to discuss wages and fill out the paperwork. The background check came back clear, but you'll need to take a drug test since you'll be operating heavy equipment. I can't afford a lawsuit or damages. Starting salary is in the offer letter."

"You're thorough. I'll give you that. And decisive." He flipped open the folder. "Got a—"

"Right here." In a single smooth motion, she unclipped a pen from her bib pocket and handed it to him. "Take your time reading everything. I'd rather not have to fill the job again for at least a few years. Can I get you a glass of water or some iced tea? Unsweet."

"I'm good, thanks." Despite her voice still strumming his nerve endings, he picked up the top page of the half dozen or so papers. The letters blurred until he straightened his arm and blinked twice.

"How about a pair of reading glasses?" Her visible eyebrow rose again as she reached for the overflowing basket on the counter. The change in her profile lit a spark in his belly as she gave him a clear view of the nearly shaved side of her head and a heart-shaped birthmark below her ear.

"No way." The whispered reaction spilled out of his mouth before his brain fully engaged.

She frowned at him over her shoulder, but the lack of a ring on her left hand as her fingers closed around a pair of glasses made the spark flare. "Denial doesn't prevent the need to magnify the fine print."

The pen slipped from his grip and clattered on the table. "Rosie Kovac?"

Her frown deepened. "How do you know my maiden name?"

"I think my ego just shriveled up and died." He leaned back in the chair and chuckled. "Barton Holloway. I asked you to the homecoming dance when you were a senior and I was a freshman. You said I was too young for you."

She lifted her hand to her mouth as her eyes widened, and her cheeks flushed the color of the pink carnations his grandmother had grown in her flower garden. "Bart? Oh my God. Everybody called you Simpson because you always had a crew cut that looked like— I'm sure you remember well enough without me reminding you. Your hair is longer now.

And the beard. You're a lot better looking than Bart Simpson as an adult. Maybe I should've said yes."

A belly laugh rumbled out of him, the first of its kind for a long time, and he swiped at his watering eyes. "You definitely should've. I had it so bad for you."

A wide smile spread across her face, reaching her pretty brown eyes.

Finally in control of his laughter, he returned her grin. "Your hair's a lot shorter now, but I like it. It fits the girl I knew back then."

"Thank you." She shoved the long side away from her cheek and lifted her chin. "My daughter thinks I'm trying to relive my youth."

His insides twisted unexpectedly. "So, you're married?"

"God, no." Her expression morphed into a reflection of pure horror. "Divorced. For a long time. You?"

"Divorced." He shrugged, not sure why that fact still bothered him. He sure as hell didn't have feelings for either of his ex-wives, unless he counted disgust. "Twice. Six years since the second one."

She closed the short distance to the table and sat across from him. "That's rough. Was it because you were on the road a lot? Some people need a lot of attention."

"Indirectly, I suppose. They both liked when I was gone. It made keeping a boyfriend on the side easier." The admission drew a scowl from Rose, but he rubbed his palms on his jeans instead of reaching to smooth away the anger lines around her mouth. "The worst part was asking my doctor to test me twice. You can't be too careful, even when you've been using protection all the time, but that was humiliating."

"I can only imagine. My ex was just a shitty husband and a shittier father. Always shirking his responsibilities. Never showing up for Beau's and Meg's birthdays and school events. He still—" She shook her head, making her hair fall across her cheek again. "Never mind. I'm sure you don't want to hear me rant about delinquent child support and non-parenting."

"I'm sorry. He sounds like a real loser." Barton picked up the pen again and tapped it against the file. "How old are your kids?"

"Twenty and eighteen. Meg's a freshman at Miami of Ohio and Beau's a junior at Ohio State." Rose's sudden smile seemed to hold a bit of wistfulness. "I'm an empty-nester most of the time now. Of course, that means I can have wild parties at my house any time I want."

Unable to contain his grin, he chuckled. "Still getting into trouble, huh?"

"Causing trouble, you mean." She waggled her eyebrows and snorted. "I have too many bills and too much work to do to be the instigator anymore. At least Beau has a part-time job that helps cover his tuition and Meg has three scholarships. Trying to keep the farm going and running the lumberyard, on top of paying for their housing? I need you to take the delivery driver job so I don't have to try to find time to do it. Plus, it doesn't gain me anything by trading a salary that's in the budget for exhaustion and the possibility of late deliveries. I can't lose those accounts."

Determined to make both their lives a little easier, he donned the too-small reading glasses she'd set on the table and focused on the paper in his hand again. "Unless the pay sucks, I want the job. Between the aches and pains I already had and the new ones that keep appearing out of nowhere, my body can't take eighteen hours a day on the road anymore. Getting old is for the birds."

"Speak for yourself. Maybe you're old, but I'm not." The

teasing in her sexy voice made his heart pitter-patter and his dick harden like it was thirty years younger.

He didn't dare glance up and risk letting her see the same infatuation he'd suffered from in high school. "I doubt you'll ever be old. Give me a few minutes to read through everything and fill out the paperwork. You don't happen to know of any local apartments or duplexes for rent, do you? Or a cheap house for sale that I can fix up?"

"Not much in the way of rentals in Bell, but I can ask around about fixer-uppers." Her chair screeched on the hardwood floor and then he caught movement out of the corner of his eye as she rose. "I'll check the real estate listings while you finish."

"Thanks." Silence surrounded him as he read and signed the contract and forms, but it wasn't uncomfortable. Her presence permeated his skin, soothing the muscle twinges and exhaustion. The long-forgotten flame obviously hadn't burned itself out, despite all the time that had passed and the experiences that had made him weary and wary of women.

Unfortunately, she was now his boss. Fortunately, he would now spend his nights at home rather than on the road, even if he'd rather spend them with this all-too-intriguing incarnation of his dream girl.

CHAPTER TWO

"Truth."

Rose Chambers slipped her insulated mug into the armrest cupholder and then rotated her hotdog stick, letting her friend stew for a full minute before unfolding the square of paper she'd drawn from the bowl next to her feet. "Okay, are you ready?"

Bits of gooey marshmallow decorating her mouth and her fingertips, Cerise Wethers nodded.

Sienna, Poppy, and Scarlet—their peri- and full-blown menopausal friends—sat with rapt attention in their chairs, clearly anxious to know what question she had to answer.

Light from the rechargeable lantern behind her revealed the handwritten words as Rose flattened the sharp folds. Adjusting her reading glasses, she thanked her lucky—and unlucky—stars she hadn't been asked this question. That would be downright embarrassing. "Oh, this is a good one. What's the highest number of orgasms you've had in a single sexual encounter with a real person? Not a toy. And list how they happened."

A grin sliding across her lips, Cerise eased the second

marshmallow from its roasting prongs and then opened wide for the whole lightly browned confection. Several slow licks of her fingertips followed as she seemed to weigh her numerous experiences. "Hmm. Well, let's see. Despite being a lazy-ass douchebag who flunked the class, a guy from undergrad advanced microbiology gave me simultaneous clitoral and vaginal orgasms with his mouth and fingers, a second clitoral orgasm with a side of ass play, and another vaginal orgasm with his uncircumcised dick. So, four in less than twenty minutes. And even though I gave him a blow job an hour later, he thought he'd earned the right to copy my homework assignments for the entire semester. He didn't, and he got a little bent out of shape when I wouldn't have sex with him again. Now if we're talking the *best* orgasms, I have another story. Or stories, especially if toys are included."

The green-eyed monster homed in on Rose's limited sexual history and set up shop in her uterus. "Four? Hell, I've been lucky to get just one unless I'm doing it myself."

Sienna grabbed the bowl and reached inside. "My turn. Truth or dare, Poppyseed?"

A frown scrunched up Poppy's face and she shook her head. "I'm going with my gut on this one. Truth."

The paper crinkled as Sienna unfolded it, blending with the low crackle of the fire. Then her raucous barks of laughter drowned out both. She finally caught her breath and glanced toward the paper again. Her mouth curved into an uncontainable grin. "Who was the first person you engaged in mutual oral sex with? Tell a fairytale of the experience using farm words."

"A fairy tale using farm words? Fuck, I need a refill for this." Poppy held her mug under the thermos spout near her elbow. Rum-spiked cider gurgled into the oversized coffee cup, and steam rose into the chilly first-evening-of-November air. She slurped and then leaned back in her canvas chair, her thoughtful expression guaranteeing a story worthy of the game. "Here goes. Once upon a time, there was a ho named Jack Shepherd. He wanted to get laid in the henhouse, so he invited a foxy redhead named Poppy Gardner on a walk with him to see if he could cultivate her attention. His bullshit was so slick that she slipped on the straw in the barn and all her attire fell off."

A cackle came from Scarlet's direction, followed by a slightly more dignified hoot from Cerise.

Fighting her own giggles, Rose waved a hand at her friend to continue the story.

Poppy straightened in her chair and aimed an impish gaze toward each of them. "The ho raked his gaze over the Gardner as he whipped out his weasel. It grew before her eyes and dripped like a leaky hose. Then he was on top of her, licking the honey in her beehive while she sucked him like a milking machine. They sowed their wild oats until the cows came home and brought them udder satisfaction. She got a mouthful of his seed and, oh boy, did she pop his Garden Weasel like a Jack in her box! The end."

A rowdy round of applause joined their laughter, chasing away some of the pervasive emptiness in Rose's heart. Being an empty nester wasn't supposed to be this hard. She'd moved on to the next phase of her life, to the chance to be selfish for the first time in more than twenty years. Grabbing the mustard-slathered bun, she eased her slightly charred frankfurter off the prongs. "Perfect. Who needs a stick?"

Leaning back in her chair, Scarlet held out her hand. "Give it to me. I'm always up for a wiener."

Not bothering to hide her amusement, Rose offered her friend the handle end and the package of hotdogs. "That's your fiancé's business. It's a wonder the poor guy's dick hasn't fallen off."

"Don't even joke about something like that." Scarlet threaded a turkey dog onto each of the two prongs.

Poppy bounced in her seat. "I'm drawing for Scarlet. She's the only one brave enough for a dare."

"I doubt you could dare me to do anything that Nelson and I haven't already tried at least once." With the loaded roasting stick poised over the fire, Scarlet tugged her sweat-shirt zipper up to her chin. "Truth."

Sienna passed the bowl to Poppy, who pulled out a square of paper.

After a sip of her spiked cider, Poppy used her cell phone to light up the next challenge in their game. Then she cleared her throat, clearly fighting another giggle fest. "What's your favorite battery-operated boyfriend and why? Hold on while I open a blank page for notes."

Sienna followed her example. "Good idea. I haven't had a chance to run next door to BOB's during business hours to pick up a Conan yet. Can't hurt to have a backup toy-friend, am I right?"

Letting the flames lick her second and third helpings of supper, Scarlet rested her elbows on her knees. "Who says you can't use more than one at the same time? I have on numerous occasions. My favorite is the wireless sonic button I bought a few weeks before Nelson and I had phone sex the first time. It fits into a pair of crotchless underwear perfectly, so you can strap it on and free up your hands to play with your nipples or use a dildo. If I put it in just the right spot, Nelson gets a little extra action too when he's fucking me from behind. Actually, I think I might suggest it when I get home tonight."

Rose's grimace likely matched the one on Sienna's,

Poppy's, and Cerise's faces. None of them had gotten any real action for a long time, let alone a little extra. Their sighs happened in unison.

"What was that for?" Although Scarlet's attention seemed fully focused on the fire, she shook her head. "If you're tired of solo orgasms, why are you all choosing truth? Didn't I go along with your unsolicited dares not that long ago?"

Rose rolled her eyes, even though her friend wouldn't be able to see in the near darkness. "Cerise set you up with your man-toy. You would've ended up together anyway. Besides, the odds of finding a guy with the proper skill set and a tolerable personality are about one in a hundred thousand or more. You got lucky."

Scarlet aimed a smart-ass smirk in her direction. "Damn right, I got lucky. And then I got lucky some more. Sienna, you're up next. Poppy, hand me the vessel of fortunes." After a quick hand-off, she balanced the bowl on her lap and withdrew a square.

Chewing on her lower lip, Sienna stuffed her hand into the bag of Fritos. "I don't have time to run the salon and have a sex life. Truth."

A shake of her head was all the judgment Scarlet offered. "When was the last time you had sexual intercourse with a man? And was it vaginal, anal, or both? Details, woman."

"This may take a minute. I have to search my calendar." Phone in hand, their corn-chip-munching friend tapped on the screen several times. "Well, shit. It's been five years, one month, and thirteen days. Vaginal. Disappointing. Breakup sex. Also the last date I had."

"That sucks." Everybody nodded at Scarlet's assessment as she passed the bowl to the final person in the lopsided circle. "Your turn to read, sneaky blind-date arranger."

With a mischievous twinkle in her eyes, Cerise locked

Rose in a steady stare. "Okay, phone-sex operator, you're up. Truth or dare? I bet you have some interesting tales."

Her stomach alternately growling for more supper and doing jumping jacks over the thought of telling a boring truth, Rose took a too-big bite of hotdog to stall. The truth was her actual history consisted of two real-life partners in all of her fifty years—and hundreds of faked orgasms for her jackass of an ex, the loser she'd slept with to celebrate her divorce, and the people who supported her second source of income after she'd gone a year and a half without a child support payment. Being the best at pretending to enjoy sex wasn't exactly something to brag about.

Pathetic.

She slowly finished chewing and swallowing, hoping to convey indecision to her friends. Only one option would let her avoid lying to them, not that she really had a choice since the other alternative surely meant having sex in some form. Who had the time or energy to bump body parts after a ten-hour workday at the lumberyard, three to seven calls to her orgasms-r-us service, and the chores her little farm required?

Adventure won out over embarrassment. "Dare."

A chorus of oohs rippled around the fire ring before Cerise opened the paper she'd drawn. Her perfectly plucked eyebrows rose and she shot a glance toward each of their companions before looking directly at Rose. "Hmm. This seems a little tame for someone who regularly talks kinky stuff to get people off over the phone."

Boring's good.

Hiding her apprehension behind another bite of hotdog, Rose crossed her fingers for an easy challenge, like showing off her favorite vibrator or watching porn on the internet, but Cerise's expression gave nothing away. "Just read it already."

Her friend uncrossed her legs and recrossed them in the

opposite direction, as ladylike in a pair of jeans and hiking boots as one of her body-clinging dresses. "Ask the first eligible bachelor you see to dinner, share at least three aphrodisiacs with him, and do more than kiss him goodnight."

More than a kiss? Do I even remember how to kiss? Does handholding count? What about a hug?

I'd rather give another pint of my blood to my ex than go on a date.

"You know I'm allergic to shellfish, right?" Rose puffed out her cheeks, imitating the blowfish she'd turn into if she ate oysters, clams, or any number of other crustaceans. "Strawberries are out of season here at the North Coast of America, along with most fruits and vegetables, and store-bought never tastes as good as fresh. What else is there? Besides chocolate."

"Champagne, phallic-shaped foods, anything that makes you think about sex." Grabbing another marshmallow from the bag, Cerise gave it a squeeze. "These remind me of blow jobs when they're all warm and gooey from roasting them over a fire. And a nice filet mignon is so…meaty."

"Aren't you tired of talking about dicks and orgasms after working all day in the toy store?"

Lips pursed and eyes wide, Cerise uncrossed her legs again and pivoted in Rose's direction. "Tired of talking about sex? Never. You definitely need to get laid, woman."

Rose shook her head. "I don't have time to—"

"If you *want* it, you make time. When was your last orgasm?" Cerise frowned and threaded another pair of marshmallows onto her stick. "By any method."

All four sets of eyes bored into Rose as she fought the urge to inform her friends that particular detail was none of their business. Technically, it wasn't, but they talked bluntly and honestly about everything.

"I don't know. Maybe three months ago? Work's been super busy, and getting Meg ready for college…" She crammed the final bite of hotdog in her mouth and hoped they couldn't see the embarrassment creeping across her cheeks.

"And intercourse?" Those symmetrical dark-blonde eyebrows rose again.

Fire hotter than the one in front of her engulfed Rose's entire body, and her mouthful lodged in her throat instead of turning to ashes from the flames. She was practically a virgin compared to these women, in spite of the fact that she had two grown children.

How had this turned into truth *and* dare?

Poppy added a log to the flickering embers and then leaned back in her chair. "Come on, Rosie. It can't be that bad."

Choking down the wad of bun, Rose begged to differ. "Thirteen years. Since the week after my divorce was finalized. I went out for a drink to celebrate, picked up a guy in a bar, and had really bad sex on the bench seat of my truck. You already know slobbering Todd was terrible at taking care of my needs. I didn't even know what good sex was until I started training for HOT TALK."

Silence fell, except for the crackle of the campfire and the faint rustle of the trees.

A phone pinged, and Scarlet pulled her cell from her coat pocket. After a few swipes and taps, she stomped at a stray spark in the dirt at her feet. "First off, I think we should all agree not to set up any blind dates without her permission. Well-meaning or not, it's awkward and uncomfortable unless you're already screwing your date. That said, do you know any decent single men worth fucking? Rose? Anybody else? Thirteen years is too damn long. That poor hymen probably regenerated itself by now."

A splutter escaped and Rose didn't even try to stop it, especially since it distracted her from the image of a certain man who'd caught at least the tail end of an oral ménage à trois with one of her regulars. She refused to risk having to replace her brand-new driver, no matter how nice he seemed or how intrigued she was by that long-ago crush he'd had on her.

Yes, he's ruggedly handsome too. "I'm pretty sure that's not possible after vaginal delivery of a nine-pound baby. Nothing's the same down there after that kind of trauma."

Cerise lifted her marshmallows from the fire and turned them this way and that. "In any case, a dare is a dare. First eligible bachelor. Three sexy foods. More than a kiss. That means a minimum of second base. Cop a feel of that man's junkyard. Let him nibble those nips or groom your pussycat. Get all hot and bothered and then give yourself an orgasm when you get home if he doesn't. I'll even donate a vibrator to the cause. Do you prefer vaginal or clitoral stimulation?"

That was definitely not a question Rose had ever imagined being asked by one of her closest friends. It also wasn't one she knew the answer to.

CHAPTER THREE

BARTON HEFTED THE LAST TWELVE-FOOT TWO-BY-SIX AND slid it onto the bed of the delivery truck. His muscles protested as he bent to retrieve the bucket of decking screws, but it beat the hell out of sitting in a rig for sixteen or more hours straight with only fuel, food, and restroom stops. The first morning on his new job had been a busy one.

A pair of worn work boots appeared in his peripheral vision, stopping an arm's length or so away from him. They were too small to belong to either of the guys who manned the service desk, assisted customers, and answered the phone. That meant his boss had ventured out of her office for a breath of brisk air.

"Hey, how's it going, Barton?" His name in that husky voice sent a zip of attraction straight to his balls.

Nothing had changed in the nine days since his interview, unless growing curiosity and interest counted.

Shaking off the not-unwelcome feeling, he added the bucket to the bed before turning toward Rose. No way would she believe loading a delivery could inspire a hard-on. "Good. I have the next three orders ready to tie down. They're all small ones and within ten miles of each other, so I can make one run instead of separate trips. Then I'll get the next big order loaded before lunch."

She nodded once, making her lopsided hair wobble back and forth. Only Rosie Kovac could convince him a partial buzzcut looked good on a woman. "You're running ahead of schedule."

"Yep." He shoved his hands in his jacket pockets to help hide the lump behind his zipper. "I was just coming in to tell you I'm heading out once I call to let the customers know I'm on my way."

A quick smile accompanied her direct gaze, triggering a slight skip in his pulse. His infatuation clearly hadn't waned at all in the last thirty-plus years.

She brushed a wayward strand of hair from her face and gave another nod. "They'll appreciate the heads-up. How's the house-hunting going? Find anything close to Bell?"

"Not yet. I checked out eight or nine last week and went to a few open houses yesterday afternoon, but most of the properties are out of my price range. I'm meeting a real estate agent to see a new listing at lunchtime." He shifted his weight to his right leg to ease a sudden stitch of pain in his left hip. Hopefully, the aches would lessen as he became more active, because forty-six wasn't that old, damn it. "She didn't have much in the way of details, so we'll see."

"Good luck." She hesitated, as if she had something else to say. Her cheeks flushed pink, but the cold was more likely responsible than shyness or embarrassment. Rose had never had a shy bone in her body, including his, which was definitely the wrong direction for his brain to take. She tugged up her collar. "I, uh… I'll ask around, in case somebody's thinking about selling. Then you can get a jump on it before the listing goes up."

Still struggling against his attraction to her, he willed his mind to cooperate. Thinking about bones and jumping wasn't helping the erection issue. What was he—fourteen again? "Okay. That'd be great. Thanks. Oh, and I'd consider renting for a few months until something comes on the market. Anything to keep from having to commute forty-five minutes to and from work every day."

"Good to know." Again, she stared at him without speaking for several long seconds. "Drive safely."

"You bet."

She tromped back toward the main building, her hair flip-flopping in time with her steps and her long legs making him wonder how they'd feel wrapped around his waist. Despite swearing off the opposite sex since his last girlfriend had dumped him, he couldn't stop his fascination with her. She was still as gorgeous and sexy and as honest and blunt at fifty as she'd been at eighteen.

Honesty was a quality he could live with, but this job would finally give him a chance to enjoy an evening at home and nights in his own bed, even if that meant sleeping alone.

Determined to make the best possible impression, he fastened the tie-downs and double-checked to be sure the load was secure. Then he climbed in the cab and referred to the purchase order for the numbers to call the customers on this circular route.

A little more than two hours later, he propped his Harley on its kickstand at the address the agent had texted him. A ranch on the slightly overgrown corner lot sat about dead center between half a dozen pink-ribboned survey stakes. At the back of the house, a gaping hole seemed to lead into a basement or crawlspace. A large sign near the front door told him and everyone else to keep out.

Tires crunched on the gravel behind him in the cul-de-sac

and a car door shut a few seconds after the engine cut out. "Mr. Holloway? I'm Vanessa Cartwright. We spoke on the phone earlier today."

He turned and extended his hand to greet the agent. "Good to meet you. Call me Barton."

"Barton, thanks for meeting me. I looked up the details after our call, and I'm afraid this property may not be what you're looking for." Pursing her lips, she handed him a sheet of paper with a gloved hand. "It's two lots, with the home straddling the property line where they meet. Half the residence is on one side and half is on the other, and only the part on the left is for sale. Apparently, the only access to the home is in the back through the crawl space. And the front isn't for sale."

He blinked at her and then down at the MLS printout she'd given him. None of the description made sense. "'Selling only part of the home on the two-lot parcel. This equals approximately half the home. The front half of the home is owned by another person and isn't for sale, so do not enter please.' I'm not sure I understand. How can you sell half a house? And what's to stop the other owner from entering the half that's for sale?"

"Foreclosure on a loan. Possibly a divorce, with the home equally divided during the proceedings." His other question evidently didn't require a response since she didn't so much as acknowledge it.

"That must've been one hell of a divorce." Returning the printout to the woman who'd wasted half of his lunch hour, he sighed. Why hadn't she told him she wanted to show him half a house on the phone? "Thanks, but I think I'll keep shopping."

She shrugged, as if inconveniencing him was no big deal.

"Please let me know if you'd like to see any other properties."

So you can waste more of my time? He barely stopped the thought from slipping out. A little politeness had never killed him, and blaming her wouldn't help him find a house faster. "Yeah. Sure. Well, I better get back to work."

Not bothering with more than an obligatory half smile, he returned to his bike and kick-started the engine. The smooth rumble invited him to spend the rest of his lunch hour cruising the backroads around the small town, but his stomach wouldn't appreciate being ignored for long, especially after a morning of more physical exertion than he was used to.

The ride back to Bell Lumber gave him a few minutes to consider his limited options if he didn't find a local place to live soon. The inevitable winter weather would arrive soon this close to the snow belt, and his mode of transportation needed an upgrade to something warmer and less treacherous to maneuver on snowy and icy roads. He could use some of the money from selling his rig to buy a car, but he'd planned on that windfall to put a decent down payment on a house and to finance a few updates to his bungalow before he turned it into a rental property. Did everybody want to live in a small town these days?

The only other viable alternative meant continuing to make the trek from Rootstown every day. While driving forty-five minutes was the blink of an eye compared to years of long-haul trips, he wanted a place that felt more permanent. Not much had anchored him in his life, other than knowing everything was temporary.

Rosie's truck was gone from its spot when he pulled into the parking lot, sparking a twinge in his gut that made him shake his head. Some old habits died a slow and awkward death, only to be resurrected by a familiar smile thirty-two years later. He needed another relationship like he needed a flat tire in the middle of a west Texas desert. Marriage brought out the worst in people, especially when they weren't fully committed to the person they'd married. Neither he nor Rose had experienced a good one.

O for three.

It hardly seemed like a good sign, not that he had any intention of exchanging vows and rings a third time—charm or no charm.

After a quick lunch in the employee break room, he patted his pockets for his phone, his keys, and his wallet. Then he headed out front to the service desk to grab the delivery clipboard from where he'd rehung it before visiting today's no-way-in-hell property listing.

Rose and her pretty smile greeted him as he rounded the counter, triggering a weird sensation in his chest. "How did the house tour go?

He pulled in a breath to ease the flutter and let it out slowly. "It was a waste of time. Something about a foreclosure or a divorce. Anyway, only half the house was for sale."

"Half? Like the basement but not the first floor? Or the back but not the front?" Her confused expression exactly matched his gut's reaction when the agent had shared those details. "How do you sell half a house?"

"Good question. I have no idea." He reached for the clipboard to give his hands something to do. "I'm not buying. It's a whole house or nothing for me."

"I wouldn't have thought finding a place to live here would be so hard." Sliding a box of order forms toward the printer, she moved a step away from him. "We'll find something for you soon. I talked to Sienna and she said she'd ask her clients at the salon. You remember Sienna Monroe, don't you? She and Poppy and I got into trouble together in high school."

Her playful grin sparked another quiver in his chest, making the necessary task of breathing without looking like a dorky freshman more difficult. "Sienna Monroe. Didn't she moon the principal after a football game or something?"

Rose's eyes sparkled as she barked a laugh. "Yep. Senior night football game. I'll have to tell her that's how you remember her."

"Well, I just heard about it. I didn't actually see her do it." A flush of heat crept up his neck. "My mom made me come straight home after the games, even when we won."

"Is she still teaching kindergarten?" A moment of deep thought came and went on her face. "Yikes. I just did the math in my head. She must be retired by now. Sometimes I forget how old I am."

"You know what they say. Fifty is the new forty, or something like that. She retired seven or eight years ago and moved next door to my little brother in Cambridge to do the grandma thing." He shifted the clipboard to his other hand and snagged the truck key from the hook under the counter. "I better get going. The Cortez Homebuilders order will take two trips, and I still have another big delivery after that."

She nodded once, sending her hair swaying back and forth again. "Simon's crew'll help you unload at the site. It's new construction and they have the equipment to move the trusses where they want them."

"Good to know." With a wave, he walked toward the side door where he'd parked the loaded truck.

"Oh, and Barton? Come find me when you get back from the run to Mosquito Lake."

"Will do." His stomach got into the act this time as his brain wandered off in the same direction his heart wanted to go. Funny how seeing her again had reignited that long-forgotten crush.

The drive to the next delivery site forced his attention to the road, even though his thoughts meandered off into fantasy territory again. He maneuvered past a backhoe, a pair of cement mixers, and a trio of gravel-laden dump trucks when he arrived at what looked like a new neighborhood consisting of modest-sized ranch and Cape Cod homes. The Cortez Homebuilders sign at the entrance proclaimed the entire development sold out. That seemed to be the case for every inhabitable house within fifteen miles of Bell.

A clean-shaven man in a hardhat and a suit waved him toward a wide gravel drive leading to a tarp-covered lot next to a single-wide mobile home that designated itself the office. Before Barton managed to line up the truck so he could back into the obvious drop-off spot, a crew of half a dozen workers exited the trailer. They stood at the ready when he shut off the engine, and the man who'd directed him to the off-load location waited as he climbed out of the truck.

"The guys'll have you unloaded in no time." An easy smile slid across the businessman's face as he extended his hand. "Simon Cortez. You must be Barton Holloway. My assistant took your call."

Tucking his work gloves under his arm, Barton shook Cortez's hand. "Good to meet you. I'll have the second load out by three o'clock."

"I appreciate it. We've had good framing weather, so we're running through lumber faster than usual." Simon pulled his cell from his pants pocket and glanced toward the screen. "Gotta take this call. Tell Rose I said hi."

A niggle of something between annoyance and jealousy tried to stick in Barton's craw, but he swallowed the feeling. She was his boss and they weren't in high school anymore.

Besides, whether or not she had a boyfriend was her business —like the phone-sex conversation he'd overheard.

He turned toward the crew to help. "You bet."

Three more hours of physical exertion did little to banish the unexpected green-eyed beast that made his heart ache the same way it had when she'd turned down his invitation to the dance and accepted another offer. If anything, the monster tried to burrow deeper, but he refused to be that guy. Who she dated, married, slept with, or had phone sex with was irrelevant, and he had no right to be jealous. Hell, he wasn't even in the market for another relationship.

His heart begged to differ as he knocked on the jamb of her open office ten minutes before closing time.

She looked up from the laptop on her desk and gestured him inside. Her tightly pursed lips thinned even more when he sat across from her and propped his left boot on his right knee.

Sucking in a slow breath, he willed away the roiling in his gut. "Is something wrong? I triple-checked every order."

Her shoulders sagged. "I didn't mean to make you think you screwed up. You didn't. In fact, Simon's assistant called a little while ago to tell me I better keep you around. Prompt, polite, professional. It's not easy to impress a perfectionist. Anyway, I was wondering if you have supper plans. I've got this…project I'm hoping you can help me with."

CHAPTER FOUR

A PROJECT*?*

The only project Rose needed to work on was herself.

She folded her hands in her lap and half hoped Barton said he already had other plans. That would be the easy way out. Then she could simply inform her friends she'd struck out with the eligible man the challenge required her to proposition, not to mention the first and only one she might consider.

He dropped the booted foot he'd rested on his knee to the floor and stared at her until she was sure the next sentence out of his mouth would include words to the effect that he didn't want to date her, was only interested in being friends, or would have to quit if she didn't take no for an answer.

After a slow and silent exhale, he licked his lips and lowered his gaze toward her desk. "I eat by myself a lot, so I'd enjoy the company. Were you thinking of eating out? Because unless you put something in a crockpot this morning, I know you haven't had time to cook."

Eating out. How many times have I heard and used that description in a phone call?

Heat crept from between her shoulder blades to her neck. Why did her mind have to veer off in that direction? "I was thinking something easy, like throwing a couple steaks on the grill, microwaving some potatoes, and putting together a salad. Carrot cake for dessert?"

His tongue snuck out again for another slow lick, triggering a sudden twinge between her thighs. "Supper sounds great, but you have to let me help. Do you have stuff to make garlic bread? If not, I can stop by the store on my way to your place."

Caught off guard by his offer, she fought the urge to round the desk and kiss him. No man but her son had ever offered to share meal prep responsibilities with her, and Beau often brought pizza when he came home so neither of them had to cook.

She leaned back and crossed her ankles beneath the chair to make acting on the impulse more difficult. Hopefully, it would also help her brain focus on the conversation instead of the disconcerting tingling where the center seam of her jeans pressed against her body. She squeezed her knees together, but that compounded the problem. *Focus, woman.* "Garlic bread sounds terrific, if it's not too much trouble to carry a baguette on your bike."

"No trouble at all. I have a storage compartment in the back." A pleased smile peeked out from the scruffy growth on his jaw and upper lip, making her brain contemplate how his beard would feel on her skin. "I guess I'll meet you at your house in about a half an hour."

She managed a nod as he rose. "Half an hour."

His easy gait out of her office spoke of a man comfortable in his own skin, the same impression she'd gotten when she'd seen him sitting on his motorcycle in his black leather jacket Saturday evening before he left. He portrayed the bad-boy image quite well, even if he'd only shown her his good side—so far. He paused at the doorway, looked back at her over his shoulder, and widened his smile before disappearing into the break room.

Her insides trembled, warning her to proceed with caution. She didn't have the time or the energy for more than a fling. She couldn't afford to lose her new driver, either. Why the hell hadn't she suffered the momentary embarrassment of a truth question and saved herself the complications of a dare?

The possibility of telling her friends she'd reached second base with a stranger without actually doing it filtered into her thoughts as she locked up, but Poppy and Sienna would see right through a lie. They would spot her fib a mile away through thick fog in the middle of a night with no moon. That was the trouble with knowing people their whole lives and getting into mischief with them.

Ten minutes later, Rose exited the lumberyard and climbed out of her truck to secure the gate with her thoughts still spinning. As she punched in the code, her phone buzzed against her hip. An involuntary fullness in her heart distracted her from the dilemma raging in her head. Her standing closing-time date never missed every Monday. "Hi, Meg. How are your classes going? Did you have fun when Em came to visit?"

"Hey, Mom. Everything's great. We pigged out on junk food and talked about all the adulting we've been doing since August. God, I miss seeing her every day. And you, of course. Texting just isn't the same, but Thanksgiving break is coming up soon and Christmas not long after that. How about you? Did you go to the Halloween party at The Ringer? Did you wear a costume?"

Rose switched to speaker and set her cell in the cup holder, thankful Beau hadn't spoiled his sister's friend weekend with news of their father's latest mishap. "Yep. I dressed up in a Spandex dress, thigh-high boots, and lots of makeup. Some drunk loser made a pass at me, and he about peed his pants when Scarlet told him he was trying to pick up a cross-dresser. Everybody started singing 'Lola.' Fun times with the gang."

Boisterous laughter filled the cab. "That's hilarious! I'm glad you had a good time. Did you meet any nice guys?"

"Uh, no. Definitely not." She flipped on her turn signal to head out of town, debating how much to tell Meg about Todd's accident. "So... Your dad... I had to leave the bar early Friday night to go donate blood. He cut himself pretty badly and needed a transfusion. He's going to be fine, but I thought you should know."

"Oh my God, what did he do now?" An eye-roll came through loud and clear.

"I have no idea. Something about pole vaulting over culvert pipes?"

"Was he stoned? Who does stupid crap like that?" Meg huffed a sigh. "I'm glad I got my intelligence from you and not from the di—"

"No name-calling. He may be far from perfect, but he's still your dad." The words tasted gross in her mouth. Todd didn't deserve defending or the title of father. "Do you know what day you'll be coming home for Thanksgiving?"

"You know, changing the subject won't change my feelings about him. He's a good-for-nothing jerk who takes advantage of your kind heart, and he's never acted like anything more than an absent sperm donor. You need to stop saving him from himself."

The sun glinted off her mailbox in the distance,

welcoming Rose home. "He can't pay thirteen years of back child support if he's dead."

Meg's grunt conveyed her feelings on that particular topic. "As if he ever will anyway. I don't have class on Wednesday, so Bo-Bo is picking me up Tuesday afternoon."

"I can't believe he still lets you call him that."

"Let? He knows he can't stop me. Besides, I think he likes being the protective big brother."

The truth in the statement triggered a burst of love. "He does. Maybe you should start asking him for spending money instead of dipping into your savings."

"Ha! He doesn't love me that much! You must be home by now. Go eat some supper and relax with a movie or a bath. I love you, Mommy."

Rose's eyes stung and her nose prickled. "I love you too, Meg-pie. Talk to you soon."

"Yep."

The line went silent as Rose pulled into the detached garage, leaving her alone with her watery eyes and a full heart. She swiped at her tears as she slid out of her pickup, more grateful than ever for her kids—her ex's one shot at redemption.

A gentle rumble greeted her when she pressed the garage door opener and stepped outside. The sound was the perfect accompaniment for the twisty-twirly feeling in her belly at the sight of her biker dinner-date. Barton had grown into a much better man than her date to the homecoming dance all those years ago. What if she'd said yes? What if she'd overlooked the fact that he was a freshman and she was a senior? What if…

Her thoughts got lost in no man's land as he lowered the kickstand and swung his leg over the seat. Then he took off his helmet, hung it on the handlebar, and ran his fingers through his wavy brown hair. Every motion seemed choreographed to seduce her into thinking she could kiss him, cop a feel of those thighs, slide into third base, and head for home —all without any consequences.

She would have to keep her hands and mouth to herself. She would also have to lie to her friends about making out with him and feeling him up, because she couldn't afford to fire the lumberyard's most competent driver in decades or have him quit.

His long pace ate up the forty or so feet between them and he held up a loaf of Italian bread. "We got lucky. Last one in the bakery section."

She donned a tight-lipped smile and waved him toward the side door to keep from telling him getting lucky should entail bumping body parts instead of snagging the last loaf of fresh bread. Damn it, her friends were going to pay for this horrible idea.

The heavy footfalls of work boots trailed her, reminding her of his height and breadth. Not many men Sasquatch-ed over her five-nine frame.

He cleared his throat when they reached the porch steps. "I forgot to tell you earlier. Simon Cortez said to tell you hi."

Shoving her key into the lock, she didn't even try to disguise a frown or hide her eye-roll. "Don't get me wrong. Simon's a nice enough guy, but he doesn't like to take no for an answer."

Barton's growl behind her caught her by surprise. "He isn't nice if he won't accept no from a woman."

"Oh, not like that!" She whipped around, and he stood so close that her nose practically touched his beard. Somehow, her hand had landed on his chest. She lowered it as she tipped her chin up and then scrubbed her wayward palm against her jeans, but his fresh fall-air scent lingered in the air. Despite having no room to step back from him, his size made her feel safe instead of trapped. "He wants to be a silent partner in Bell Lumber so I can expand and compete with larger suppliers in the area. Of course, he'd have the side benefit of being able to eliminate the middleman expense for his construction business. And profit from it."

Had she sounded as breathy to him as she had to herself?

His eyes locked on hers and held her tight in a way that unexpectedly comforted and aroused her. "What do you want to do?"

That was a loaded question if she'd ever heard one. A dozen naughty ideas pounced at once, and all of them triggered bodily reactions like Todd and her HOT TALK line never had.

She fought to turn toward the door and steer her thoughts back to the real conversation. "My father started the company almost fifty years ago. It's been mine since he retired, and I like being in charge. The influx of capital would be handy, but it's not worth selling out."

"And Cortez is pushing you to part with a percentage of the business. Sounds a little sleazy to me."

"Not really. He's a bit of a workaholic, and he likes the challenge of trying his hand at new business opportunities." Casting a glance at her guest, she walked into the house. "I can see why you think it sounds underhanded, but his intentions are good."

"I hope so." He took two steps into her kitchen and halted. "Should I leave my boots here? I kicked the mud off as best I could after the last delivery, but some of it's still stuck in the tread."

"By the door's fine. Of course, if you track mud all over the place, I'll have to make you sweep and mop. Then I won't have to." She tossed a smirk at him and shrugged as she unzipped her coat. "Or you could pay for a housekeeper. Take your pick."

His belly laugh washed over her in rush of goose bumps and tingles. "Spoken like a woman who's raised a teenage boy. My mom used to say the same thing."

"So did mine, but I was the one leaving a trail of destruction behind." A stealthy peek behind her when she bent to untie her own boots gave her a glorious view of his jeans-clad ass.

"Well, you did have a reputation for causing trouble." He caught her gaze in his before she could look away, and one eyebrow rose toward his forehead. "Can I ask you a question?"

Heat flooded her cheeks, but she refused to hide her reaction. "Sure. Doesn't mean I'll answer it, though."

"Fair enough." His lips curved into a wide smile, increasing her sexual temperature several more degrees. "Is tonight's supper invitation a friends-catching-up thing? Or is it a date?"

How could a middle-aged man be so damn cute?

"That's two questions." Glad for an opportunity to throw around a little sass, she returned his grin. Her boot clunked on the tile floor after a firm tug on the heel. "And I'm not sure yet. Which do you want it to be?"

He toed off his own boots, without breaking eye contact. "Job-wise? The friends thing. I know it was just my first day, but I like working at Bell Lumber and I don't really want to look for something else. I especially don't want to go back to driving a semi. Now if I'm being honest with myself, I hope it's a date. My stomach feels an awful lot like it did every time I saw you in the hall outside Mrs. Brewer's classroom. Sort of like somebody's making pretzels with it. I like pretzels, though."

"Yeah, well, your stomach is in good company." She yanked off her other boot and dropped it next to its mate, torn between hightailing it to the farthest reaches of the Earth and dragging him off to her bedroom for a week or two. "I haven't decided how I feel about that yet, so let's play it by ear for now. Okay?"

"Works for me." After placing his leather jacket on the hook next to hers, he snagged the plastic grocery bag with the loaf of bread sticking out of the top from where he'd hung it on the doorknob. Four long strides carried him to the sink. "What do you want me to do first? Besides wash my hands."

Would he kiss her if she asked him to? Or would an attempt to diffuse the attraction backfire?

The people who called her sex line stated exactly what they wanted and got down to business. This uneasy tension with unknown expectations reminded her of being in high school and all the angsty drama that went with it. She hadn't reached middle age with a failed marriage under her belt to play at that nonsense.

Closing the distance between them in her stocking feet, she gathered every ounce of daring she could muster before she changed her mind. "I want you to kiss me first. Like you mean it. And then we'll go from there."

CHAPTER FIVE

"LIKE I MEAN IT?" THE WORDS CAME OUT ROUGH, BUT Barton bulldozed through his nervousness. The moment he'd unknowingly waited thirty-two years for had finally arrived. His feelings for Rosie Kovac had lain dormant, not faded or gone away with time. "I don't usually go around kissing women—and definitely not with the sole intention of getting laid. Especially you."

Rose draped her arms around his neck as she raised to her tiptoes. "Why especially me?"

Her husky question skittered along his nerve endings, assuring him his imagination had never done justice to this moment. He rested his hands on her waist to hold her in place, close enough to touch but not so close that he couldn't resist touching more of her. "High school was a long time ago, and I'm realizing not much has changed when it comes to… Let's just say I'd still ask you to the dance."

Her eyes lit up with something other than her normal mischievousness, hinting that his interest pleased her. "What if I want more than a dance?"

Not trusting himself to answer without sounding like a

horny teenager, he lowered his mouth to hers, first in a whisper-light touch to be sure she truly wanted more and then going back to savor the softness of her lips after her breathy sigh. When she welcomed him inside, she tasted as sweet and fruity as the lemon drops she used to sneak in study hall—exactly the way he'd dreamed, only better because it was finally real. A tentative stroke of her tongue along his triggered a groan to go with the heavy ache in his balls and the need to adjust the rapidly stiffening cock in his jeans.

A simple kiss had never done that before.

She leaned closer, pressing her breasts into his chest and her lower belly against his erection. Her low hum vibrated through his jaw as she raked her fingers through his hair. Very adult sensations joined the first-crush feelings waking in his memory at the touch of her fingertips on his scalp and then his neck and jaw. His fantasies of kissing her had never reached these heights of desire and physical need.

He slid his palm lower to cup her shapely ass before his brain engaged, but logic insisted he slow the hell down before they got too carried away. A make-out session seemed infinitely smarter than what his dick wanted. Untangling their tongues and easing his mouth away, he rested his forehead against hers to catch his breath. Good or bad, his hand refused to budge from its current location. "Wow. I don't usually grope on a first date. Maybe we should save some dessert for after supper."

Her kissable lips curved upward and her warm breath feathered through his beard and across his chin with each uneven exhale. "Probably. I wasn't expecting a fire in the kitchen."

A laugh tickled his throat, but that wasn't necessarily a terrible thing. Neither of his marriages had included much laughter and they hadn't ended well. Was he a fool for wondering if the third time would be the charm? Was he asking for more trouble? Or was she the woman he should've waited for? "Just a few sparks. I think we have it under control for now."

"For now." She pressed a light kiss to his cheekbone and then slipped from his hold, triggering a mix of relief and disappointment. As she sauntered toward the fridge, she looked back at him over her shoulder. "I like you, Barton Holloway."

He didn't bother to fight the elation thrumming through his body and mind. His heart beat strong and steady in his chest and hope surged through his veins, despite the risks of dating his boss. "I like you too, Rosie Kovac."

"Good to know." His accidental use of the name he'd known her by in school didn't seem to bother her, but her already flushed cheeks turned a slightly deeper shade of pink. She transferred a brown paper-wrapped package from the freezer to the microwave and tapped a few buttons to start the defrost cycle. "I'll preheat the grill and scrub the potatoes while you make the salads and garlic bread. There's a tub of garlic butter in the door of the refrigerator and a bag of salad and tomatoes in the produce drawer."

"Got it." Glad for the distraction, he gathered the supplies, utensils, and dishes he needed when she headed out to the patio off the adjacent side of the kitchen. As easily as he could picture spending a lifetime with her, he needed to step back and keep a tight rein on his tendency to jump in the deep end without knowing how to swim in woman-infested waters.

Rose stepped inside a few minutes later and closed the sliding door behind her. "The grill should be ready in about ten or fifteen minutes. Did you find everything okay?"

"Yep." Keeping his eyes trained on the knife and bread

on the cutting board, he sliced off a wide heel and set it aside. Even so, his pulse picked back up again from her nearness.

She moved into his peripheral vision and stopped a few feet away at the sink. Running water drowned out the thudding of his heartbeat in his ears. "I hope you like garlic salt and Tabasco. I seasoned the steaks before I put them in the freezer. My mom always did it that way to save time. How do you like yours cooked? Still mooing, pink center, or charred to a crisp?"

He couldn't help chuckling at her choices. "Pink's good."

"That makes my life easier. My son wants it practically raw and my daughter likes it too done to chew. When they were tall enough to stand at the grill without burning themselves, I told them they had to cook their own or never complain about undercooked or overcooked meat again." She scrubbed a vegetable brush over the potato in her hand, seemingly recovered from their amazing first kiss. "It'll be nice to make two the same way for a change. How about salad dressing? Ranch or—" Her phone buzzed against the counter on the opposite side of the sink. "Sorry, got to grab this. It'll just take a minute."

With half a dozen thick slices of bread ready for buttering, he nodded and slipped the rest of the loaf back into the bag while she dried her hands.

Then she tapped the screen, putting the call on speaker. "Hey, Cerise. I found your earring on the bathroom floor this morning. I meant to text you at lunchtime, but I got busy and forgot. You know how that goes."

The musical ping of what sounded like coins clinking together filled the kitchen. "Great, thanks. Actually, I was calling to see if you made any progress on your dare. It's been a week. Did you ask a hunky guy to dinner yet?"

Rose gasped and grabbed for her cell, but it slid out of her reach. She scrambled for it again.

The woman's voice held no small amount of determination. "You need a man-induced org—"

Despite the sudden cutoff, Barton had no trouble figuring out the intended last word. Was that the reason Rose had invited him to supper—to have sex with him? Or at least score a big O?

Her eyes met his and she turned fourteen shades of red from her forehead to the generous strip of skin showing at the neckline of her long-sleeved tee, making the answer perfectly clear. Then she glanced away and raised her phone to her ear. "I have to go. Company. I'll call you later."

A long stretch of silence filled the kitchen, but he let it hover around them instead of letting his jumping conclusions turn into accusations. At least his dick had ducked into hiding from the likelihood of another failed attempt at a relationship.

She stuffed her cell in her pocket, braced her hands against the edge of the counter, and lowered her head until her hair blocked his view of her face. "I'm really sorry. I don't embarrass easily, but… God, that had to sound *so* bad. My friends and I played this stupid game about a week ago. I accepted a silly dare because it seemed better than telling a pitiful truth. Then they started suggesting aphrodisiacs I should serve my date and told me I had to get to second base since the dare included more than just kissing him goodnight. But I swear I didn't ask you to a supper seduction. The rest… I was going to lie about the orgasm. Seriously. I'm no prude, but I'd rather not have sex with a stranger. Real sex."

Her apology and explanation took more effort to process than he usually expended for the daily crossword puzzle app on his phone. Of course, he didn't have any experience with the women in his life telling him they were sorry. He couldn't even wrap his mind around encouraging a fifty-year-old female—a mother, no less—to go that far on a first date. Didn't her friends know how shifty most men were?

His mouth opened and closed twice before he managed to find any words. "Are Poppy and Sienna the friends who dared you to do this?"

She nodded, but her face was still hidden by her hair. "And Scarlet, the new mechanic in town. No, not new exactly. She's been back in Bell for almost a year. She grew up here. And Cerise. She owns the adult toy store two blocks down from the grocery store. BOB's Pleasure Palace."

He swallowed a retort that her choice of friends hadn't improved since high school. Who was he to judge, considering he didn't have any buddies he could rely on in a pinch except on the road? Or even meet up with for a beer?

She groaned. "Shit. You're probably thinking I'm a dick tease after the conversation you heard the other night. It was phone sex. Not real. Not for me anyway. I run a HOT TALK franchise line to help pay the bills. Please don't tell anybody."

The three-way he'd overheard Saturday evening made sense now, even if he didn't like the idea of other men—or women—getting off to the sound of her husky voice while she told them all the sex-related things they wanted to hear. Fortunately, her threat to fire him hadn't made a repeat appearance.

"Of course I won't. It's nobody's business but yours. Back to you asking me to come for supper." He cringed at his word choice, even though he itched to find out how hot their chemistry burned. Why did every thought suddenly have a sexual connotation? "Not come. Have me for dinner. God, that's even worse. The game of truth or dare got out of hand, right?"

She shoved her hair out of her face and turned toward him. "Yes, but it's not their fault. They meant well and they wanted to take my mind off my kids being gone. I've been having a hard time living alone."

"That's understandable. They've been a big part of your life since they were born." Unable to stop himself, he moved closer and wrapped his arms around her. A sense of peace and rightness seeped into him. Where was the instinct to be careful or he'd end up back where he'd been six years ago and four years before that?

"The biggest part."

A ridiculous thought formed in his head as he tried to balance what should've been the automatic reaction to run the other direction against the need to comfort her. Would it be such a bad idea? Maybe, but he could control himself—and he trusted her. "So, I might have a solution."

Her head snapped up from its resting place against his chest. "Menopause is halfway through the front door and looking to get comfortable on the living room couch. Even if it wasn't, I'm way past the point of wanting to have another baby."

He could only gape at her for making that assumption. "No! That's not what I was going to say at all. I was thinking… What if you had another source of income? Would you be able to quit the phone-sex job? Or do you make a lot of money from it?"

"It was enough to cover groceries, clothes, and school expenses when Beau and Meg still lived at home. My ex's child support was supposed to pay for all that, and I couldn't depend on it. Now it pays for books and part of their housing costs. No other job brings in as much money for the number of hours I have to work."

"Your ex is a worthless waste of space." The verdict came

out before he could censor his response. "Sorry. I shouldn't have said that."

"No need to apologize. It's true. He's unreliable and irresponsible. The only reason I have any contact with him is the off-chance he'll win the lottery and be able to pay what he owes me."

Barton swallowed the rest of his assessment of the idiot so he could forge ahead with his somewhat selfish suggestion. "I was going to suggest that I rent a room from you if you have the space. You'd have a new income stream. Plus, I'm willing to help with the cooking and cleaning and whatever else needs done. The barn could use a coat of paint and the security light hums like a nest of angry hornets. It probably needs a new sensor."

She narrowed her eyes and pursed her lips, as if she was trying to see through a smokescreen or she suspected he had nefarious motives. "What's in it for you? Besides the possibility of getting laid?"

He let his hands fall away from her waist and put an arm's length between them. Honesty was the only way to go, despite the truth in her observation. "I could take my time finding something to buy and I'd get to spend time with you. I'm not going to lie. It feels like there's something between us. If you want to be more than friends, I would absolutely be interested, but I'm also okay with us having completely separate spaces if that's what you want."

Her expression softened. "Like frenefits? Or benefriends? I don't know the current slang for it."

He nodded in time with the thudding in his ears. "Or more, depending on what we want out of it."

"You'd be fine with a fling?" One of her eyebrows arched toward the stubble on the side of her head.

"I think we might be a little past calling it that, age-wise. Don't you?"

The frown returned. "Just because my friends and I are in our fifties doesn't mean we can't have a fling. Or a little fun. What's wrong with enjoying some hanky-panky? We're not old or dead."

He shrugged and hoped his dick wasn't listening to her talk about hooking up and fooling around. "Well, nothing, I guess."

"Then let's finish making supper and eat so we can see if a fling is worth the effort. No sex is better than bad sex." She spun toward the microwave, letting him peruse her cute ass and wonder if his skills were up to snuff.

CHAPTER SIX

To fling or not to fling.

That was only one of two big questions Rose had yet to answer. The other tempted her as much as it worried her.

No, she wasn't afraid of renting a room to Barton. His background check had come back spotless and he'd been a model employee his first day at the lumberyard. She was, however, more than a little concerned about playing house with him and keeping her heart intact. That organ had suffered a few cracks in its lifetime, the most recent of which—Meg flying the nest—had left her struggling to redefine herself without so much mother in the mix.

Her supper guest rejoined her in the living room, settling on the opposite end of the couch once again. He leaned back and stretched his long legs out in front of him. "Plates and forks are rinsed and in the dishwasher."

"Thanks, but you really didn't have to do that." Shifting into the corner, she tucked her hands between her knees to keep from reaching for him.

"Sure, I did." His relaxed smile reignited the sparks that hadn't stopped flaring off and on since he'd entered her office hours ago. "I haven't enjoyed a meal this much in a long time and carrot cake is my favorite. Great food. Great company. You shouldn't have to clean up my mess when I can do it."

"Well, thank you, even though you didn't have to take care of mine too." When had she last shared a truly enjoyable moment with a man? Had she ever? He'd simultaneously submerged her in a wonderful cocoon and forced her out of her comfort zone—or more like familiar zone since her life didn't allow for much comfort anymore.

"You're welcome." He rubbed his palms along the tops of his thighs and then pushed to his feet, probably feeling as antsy as she was. "I should get going. You probably have things you need to do. Will you think about renting me a room? No pressure about the rest."

God, how she wanted to be those hands, or at least have them on her own thighs and a few other places.

Why couldn't she?

So what if he worked for her?

They were adults, and she was capable of keeping her personal and professional lives separate. Besides, her friends were right. She deserved an orgasm from some other method than masturbation with a vibrator that suffered from neglect.

She rose and let her wants instead of her needs guide her for a change. "If you haven't found someplace by the end of the week, we'll talk more about you renting from me. The garage has an old apartment upstairs. It needs a little work, but... As for *the rest*, I'm ready if you are."

His gaze jumped to hers, but he froze mid step. Several seconds ticked by before he nodded. "You're sure? We don't have to—"

"It sounds to me like you're trying to backtrack. Are *you* sure?" Shaking off her nervousness and giving attraction free rein, she crossed to him, stopping when they were nearly toe to toe. She hoped like hell the intensity in his stare translated to desire for her and didn't mean she would end up a pile of ashes from getting burned.

"Very sure." He slipped his arm around her waist and grasped her right hand with his free left one. His eyes stayed locked on hers, exerting a pull she didn't want to resist, and a hint of a smile curved the lips that had almost seduced her into skipping supper earlier. "We could start with the dance I never got in high school."

"That sounds nice." She skimmed her fingers up his arm to his shoulder, far too aware of the muscles beneath his thermal Henley. "You know you were too young for me back then, right?"

His low chuckle tickled her ear as he swayed back and forth, barely moving his feet. "Maybe. Maybe not. Aren't feelings and compatibility more important than age? I'm not saying a difference of six or eight or ten years would be appropriate in high school, but plenty of senior guys dated freshman girls. Besides, you never seemed like the kind of person who would care much about what other people thought."

"I didn't. I don't." Her breath hitched and her thoughts scattered when his hip brushed hers. "I, uh, I guess I should've put more stock in maturity. It's lost time, and we'll never get it back or be able to relive it. It doesn't mean we have to dwell on regrets, though."

He hummed what sounded like agreement and spun them into a slow circle with a thigh between her legs. "No regrets, just a few what-ifs. I'm glad I'm here now, no matter what happens five minutes, five days, five years from now."

"Five minutes from now we could be naked and having sex." Anticipation spread from her lower belly to every erogenous zone she talked about to her clients—the places she hadn't been sure still existed in her own body.

A rumble vibrated through his chest into her as he guided her around the room. "And I'll be glad for that moment too, if it's what we both want."

She followed her instincts at the bottom of the stairway and tugged him up the steps toward her bedroom. Bravery might get her heart into trouble, but those what-ifs wouldn't hound her for the rest of her life. "I want it. I want you."

Before she reached the third step, he scooped her into his arms and carried her to the second-floor landing. "Right or left?"

Feeling more breathless than if she'd carried six loads of clean sheets, blankets, and comforters upstairs and remade all the beds, she pointed to the right. "The last room."

He hurried along the banister and then flipped the light switch with his elbow as he entered her bedroom. The matching lamps on the nightstands cast shadows over the private space she'd never shared with a husband, a lover, or even a one-night stand. It probably appeared a bit more subtle than her personality, but the soft colors and scented candles scattered on the tops of both dressers and night tables reminded her she was a woman, first and foremost.

At the foot of the bed, he slowly lowered her feet to the floor, sliding her down the solid planes of his body. God, he was hard in all the right places.

Before she could wrangle a coherent thought from her brain, he touched his lips to hers. His beard and mustache tickled her skin as he repeated the motion over and over. Each teasing brush ignited tingles along her arms and legs and every part in between.

She tightened her hold on his shoulders and deepened the next kiss. Instead of the forceful grinding against her mouth she half expected, he followed her lead, never trying to gain control. Each slow glide of his tongue promised he planned to sweep her off her feet the way he had on the stairs. If not for her grip on him and his arms around her waist, she would've melted into a puddle on the floor.

One of his hands moved upward to a spot between her shoulder blades and the other slipped into the back pocket of her jeans, upping her pulse and the heat moving through her veins. For the first time in forever, sexual need coursed through her body. The feeling of empowerment worked like a Jack and Coke without the Coke, giving her the confidence to attack the vertical line of four buttons on his chest one-handed and shove her fingers into his thick hair.

He groaned into her mouth when her fingertips grazed his skin. His hand slipped free of her pocket and he tugged at the Bell Lumber button-down shirt she'd worn all day. The long-sleeved tee was next, the motion creating a sudden draft of cool air. Then the heat from his palm spread like wildfire across her lower back.

She gasped at the overwhelming sensation, breaking their oral connection, but the loss she'd expected didn't happen.

He nibbled a path along her jaw to her ear, his rough breathing sending puffs of humid air across her neck. "I could kiss you for hours."

"Hold that thought for a sec." She eased away from him far enough to grab the hem of his Henley and help him work it over his head. Without slowing, she yanked off both of her own layers at once, leaving only her bra. "Better."

"Mm-hm." His mouth descended onto hers again as he found and released the hooks at the middle of her back.

Her near nudity should have distracted her, but need and want took over. She shrugged off the straps and cups, finally putting her skin to skin with him from the waist up. Her nipples tightened against the coarse hair on his chest, the sensations amplifying the tiny tremors zipping from her breasts to her lower belly to the ache between her thighs.

His heavy sigh brought a sudden rush of doubts and self-consciousness. Had he noticed the stretch marks zigzagging across her stomach and boobs? A litany of comebacks formed in her mind in case he had the nerve to tell her she was too imperfect.

He combed her hair away from her face and whimpered. "I don't have a condom on me, not that I expect… But I like to be prepared. Just once without is all it takes."

A mix of relief and disappointment jumbled together before her brain engaged. Poppy had given her a box of assorted novelty items from BOB's for her birthday a few months ago. Surely, it included at least a sample package of ribbed, neon, or flavored condoms. If not, she might have to resort to a sandwich bag or a rubber glove because, damn it, she refused to have the choice taken from her.

"I might have one." She tugged him toward the closest nightstand. "You check here. I'll check the other side."

Clanks and rattles came from behind her as she rounded the end of the bed, reminding her she'd stowed several vibrators and a supply of batteries in Barton's drawer. She waited until she reached the opposite side to glance his direction.

He smirked at her and continued his search. "From your friend's toy store?"

"Yes." Thankful he hadn't made a smartass remark, she crossed her fingers and pulled open the drawer that usually held an extra charging cord for her phone, spare change, and a travel-sized sewing kit.

"I'm not opposed to using them if what I do doesn't get

the job done." His gravelly voice raked over her nerve endings, inciting more interest in sex than she'd experienced in a decade or two.

"Good to know I don't have to take care of that myself." She rooted through the mishmash of furry handcuffs, silk ties, and penis-shaped candies until what felt like a trio of foil packets crinkled in her fingers. "Aha! Three of them."

His bicep flexed as he shut away her toys, drawing her attention to the toned upper half of his body. "Three. Okay."

She barely contained a fist-pump at what seemed to be his acceptance of a challenge. Instead, she tossed her find toward the pillows and knee-crawled across the bed to finish unwrapping this gift of a man. "I'm thinking we should get rid of the rest of our clothes so we can concentrate on what we're doing."

His wide grin set off another round of firecrackers in her belly. "That's the Rosie Kovac I remember. Always ready for anything."

He clearly had no idea about the fear she battled.

Unfastening the button at her waistband, she kept her gaze focused on the man about to get naked with her. "Maybe not anything, but I'm ready for you."

His smile softened and he took over undressing her. Despite her wish to hurry through that part and get to the good stuff, she savored the gentle way he eased the jeans past her hips and then laid her on the bed to pull on the hems. Then he kissed her ankles as he peeled off her socks.

She bit her cheek to keep from cringing. *God, I hope my feet don't stink after wearing work boots all day.*

With only her rattiest pair of underwear remaining, he shucked his own pants, leaving a pair of boxer briefs that left almost nothing to her imagination. His erection twitched behind the snug gray cotton, and her vaginal muscles responded in kind. "I should suit up now, in case I get distracted. More distracted. I'm not going to want to stop once I get started showing you how much I thought about kissing you and making love to you all through supper."

If she hadn't been sprawled out on her bed, she would've swooned from the desire and romance that laced his words. A grab for the pillows yielded a bright red packet with bold lettering. "'Fuck Me Now.'"

His thick brows rose almost to the hair drooping across his forehead, his eyes widened slightly, and his lips curved upward at the corners. "Yes, ma'am. Your wish is my command."

"And it says it's a large." A giggle-snort slipped out as she handed him the packet, the message face-up. "I prefer foreplay, just so you know, especially if that bad boy is as big as he looks."

He glanced away, but not before she caught a blush coloring his cheeks. "Girth is sometimes an issue."

Instead of striking fear in her vagina, his admission triggered a ripple of awareness stronger than her ex's infrequent accidental stimulation of her G-spot. She shimmied out of her undies with the worn-out elastic and then crooked her finger at him. "That's not going to be a problem. I promise. Now make my wish come true."

In a matter of seconds, he dropped his drawers, rolled on the florescent red condom, and hooked her knees over his shoulders. Then he licked a wicked path up the inside of her leg and buried his face between her thighs. His tongue found her clit on the first swipe, stealing her breath as she arched against his mouth. A low hum added to the stimulation, the steady vibrations amplifying the tingles quickly building toward her first orgasm in months.

Her eyes tried to drift closed, but his gaze locked on hers, determination and heat burning in their depths. The lust glowing in his eyes matched the level in her veins. Then a hint of satisfaction shined through and he slipped a thick finger inside her. A second one joined the first on the next smooth glide, sending her tumbling over the edge. She cried out, immersing herself in the sensation as pulsing waves overtook her.

Before she could catch her breath, he was on the bed, easing his thick cock into her and cupping her face in his palms. His lips caressed hers as he slowly filled her. "Okay?"

She was better than okay. Despite the way he stretched her to the limit, the fullness created a connection she'd never felt before. No pain or disappointment seemed to lurk on the horizon. She wrapped her arms around him, relishing the bond. "Perfect."

He kissed her, sharing the taste of her body with her, and gently rocked in and out. The easy motion belied the tension in his muscles, so she pivoted her hips to meet him, encouraging him to show her how much he wanted her, how much he had to have her right this minute.

The moment his control broke was like a shout to the world. His tongue moved in time with his cock through every frenzied thrust, his groans telling her he was as close to flying apart as she was.

He slammed into her, triggering another rush of lightheadedness and euphoria. His animalistic bellow pushed her higher than she would've thought possible, and she clung to him to keep from floating away.

Braced above her, he pressed his forehead to hers. Only their rough breathing broke the silence for several minutes.

The distinctive sound of high heels on the wood floor suddenly invaded the afterglow, and Cerise appeared in the doorway with a big grin. “Good for you, woman. Dare achieved. I came over to see if you’d made any progress and to drop off Conan. You, Mr. Lumberjack, better have given her at least two orgasms. Not fake ones, either.”

CHAPTER SEVEN

BARTON STOWED THE LAST OF THE TIE-DOWN STRAPS BEHIND the seat and climbed into the delivery truck's cab. His muscles were still getting used to loading and unloading building supplies multiple times a day and a hot shower would hit the spot, especially if Rosie joined him. That might hold him over until he moved into the garage apartment she'd agreed to rent him, although she'd made it clear she didn't expect him to sleep there every night. The clean-up and move-in work would start tomorrow. Tonight she had plans to host a get-together with her friends, and neither of them needed the speculation his presence would no doubt bring.

Heat crept up his neck. One of those friends, a petite blonde named Cerise, had caught him buck naked on top of Rose three nights ago and practically applauded him for his mutually satisfying performance in bed. Although he'd clearly earned her approval, he could've done without the audience. No way in hell could she not have heard the sex noises when she entered the house.

Shaking off his embarrassment for the umpteenth time, he shifted into gear and cast careful glances at the side mirrors, up to the rearview mirror, and back to the side mirrors again. As he reached for the gearshift, Simon Cortez exited the trailer office beside the delivery area and waved an arm at him to hold up. The other man's boots, jeans, Carhartt jacket, and the hardhat under his arm said he'd been helping his crews at the site today instead of going to business meetings and schmoozing with bankers or investors.

Barton rolled down the window and shut off the truck so he could have a conversation without yelling over the rumbling engine. It sounded like it was due for a tune-up. "Hey, Simon. How's it going?"

Cortez closed the last few feet between him and the driver's side door. "Good. We're trying to stay ahead of schedule right now, so I appreciate the extra deliveries this week. Gotta make up for the upcoming holidays and bad weather when we can."

"Not a problem. The busier Bell Lumber is, the better. For me and for Rose." Saying her name reignited the warmth in his chest that hit every time he saw or thought of her. A single night of sharing her bed and four days of working for her had confirmed what he'd suspected during his job interview. His heart still belonged to her.

"Glad to hear everything's going well. I'm headed to The Ringer after we finish up for the day. Join me for a beer and a burger?" Simon donned the hardhat and tugged a pair of work gloves from his coat pocket. "My treat. I have a business proposition for you."

Barton's eyebrows rose and he stifled a frown. Did Cortez plan to entice him away from his current employer? "What kind of proposition?"

"A little side work, if you're interested." Looking toward the work site across the street, Simon gave his hardhat a pat on his head. "About six fifteen?"

Barton nodded, willing to give the man the benefit of the doubt for the moment. Besides, the discussion might distract him from thinking about all the ways he wanted to make love to Rosie. "Sure. See you in about an hour and a half."

Without another word, the builder waved and tromped toward the house going up on the corner lot. One of the guys who'd helped unload yesterday's load of supplies met him at the road, most likely giving him a progress report.

Triple-checking his mirrors again, Barton pulled out of the delivery drive and headed back to the lumberyard. "A little side work" prompted thoughts of mafia jobs before the possibility of anything else, despite Rosie's assurance Cortez wasn't really trying to coerce her into taking on a partner. The guy seemed nice enough, but that didn't mean his motives were noble.

The fifteen-minute drive carried Barton's thoughts back to his boss, the woman he might be willing to risk a third marriage for. Third time's the charm had to become a saying for a reason, hadn't it?

Only one vehicle remained in the customer parking lot. Her truck still sat toward the back in the spot next to his Harley, the same as when they'd parked this morning. Next week, they would start riding together in her pickup—hopefully, after shared nights together all weekend. The memory of waking up beside her brought to mind the box of condoms he'd picked up at lunchtime and stowed in the storage compartment of his bike. The three she'd found in her nightstand drawer were long gone.

A chorus of feminine voices greeted him as he walked into the building through the side entrance, Rosie's huskiness standing out among them like a provocative caress along his zipper. The door to her office stood open, giving him a glimpse of a dark-haired woman in flipflops and a redhead with a pair of rubber gloves tucked in her back pocket. They turned toward him when the heavy exterior door clunked shut. Both their chins dropped and two sets of eyes widened before a pair of matching grins beamed at him.

The women looked too much like Poppy and Sienna, Rose's longtime partners in crime, to be anyone else.

After a knowing smirk at Rose, the redhead extended her hand. "Simpson! Long time, no see. I mean Barton. Sorry about that. Old habit. Look at you. You're all grown up. Poppy Gardner."

Sienna snorted and shoved her hand at him as well. "Hey, Barton. Sienna Monroe, if you don't remember me from high school. Rosie mentioned you're delivering for her."

Rose's face turned a violent shade of red as Poppy and Sienna busted a gut at the possible but highly improbable accidental implication. They obviously knew all about the night of sexual escapades earlier in the week. Good news had traveled fast among the friends—likely via Cerise, the only witness to the deed. From Rose's look of horror, she hadn't done the telling.

He swallowed to clear the tickle from his throat and shook their hands, one after the other. "Good to see you again. Rose, I just wanted to let you know I'm back from Cortez Homebuilders. Oh, and do you know where I can find the service records for the truck? It sounds like it needs an adjustment or two."

She shoved her fingers through the longer section of her hair and sighed. "There should be a folder with a log of maintenance and repairs in the middle file cabinet under the printer counter. Let me know if you need any parts in the morning and I'll order them."

After a brief nod, he escaped to the filing system around the corner, doing his best to ignore the giggles following him away from her office. A few words—big, proportionate, and wowza—carried to his burning ears, so he grabbed the labeled file and made a break for the other side of the store. Hiding among the buckets of nails, boxes of screws, and bins of brackets, he shuffled through what looked like about six years' worth of receipts.

Before he'd read through the most recent service notes, Rose's visitors strolled toward the main entrance. Both still wore wide smiles, and Poppy gave him a thumbs-up as she trailed Sienna out the door.

Rose popped her head around the mini tower of buckets. "Sorry about that. I swear to God women are just as crude about sex and men as the other way around."

"No worries." He tightened his grip on the papers to keep from pulling her close enough for a much-needed kiss. He'd missed touching her all week, but PDA at her place of business wasn't a line he was willing to cross unless she initiated it. "Want me to lock up?"

"I got it." She waved him off and crossed to the glass double doors, her long legs drawing his attention to her confident walk. Her independence added to his raging attraction. "I know you have packing to do, but I was wondering if you have time to swing by the house on your way home. The shoot-the-shit session over supper doesn't start until six-ish."

"A booty call?" He shot her what he hoped was an inviting but flabbergasted ogle.

Her laughter rang through the high-ceilinged space. "Well, I was going to ask you to help me get the old garden tractor running so you have more room in the garage for your bike, but that works too."

He returned the receipts to the folder and closed it. God, he adored this older version of his crush. "How about both? I'll follow you."

She glanced at him over her shoulder as she hurried toward her office. "Just so you know, I bought a box of condoms on my lunch break."

Watching her hips sway back and forth, he couldn't help but put a little swagger in his steps. "Great minds. I did too."

At her desk, she snickered and pulled her purse from one of the drawers. "I don't know about great, but they're definitely in agreement about the booty call."

"I got a jumbo pack. You?" He retrieved her coat from its hook, not sure whether to hand it to her or attempt holding it for her while she slipped her arms in the sleeves.

"Same." She saved him from having to make the decision by snagging it on her way past him. "Thanks. Ready to go?"

"Whenever you are."

With the coat slung over her arm, she pulled the door closed behind them. "Just need to make sure the keys are locked up."

"I did that when I got the service file. Truck's parked under the carport and I filled the gas tank after the Cortez delivery." He barely kept from running over her when she suddenly stopped in front of him.

She whirled around and stared at him for several long seconds before shaking her head. "Let's go."

"What?" He followed her to the exit. "You want to say something. I can tell."

Her shoulders tensed as she jangled her keys and pushed open the exterior door. "I'm used to having to tell everybody what to do and how to do it, so now I'm wondering what your big flaw is."

"That's easy." The late afternoon chill hit him in the face when he stepped outside. "I try to put a hundred percent into everything I do and expect the same from everybody else. Unfortunately, that doesn't usually work out very well for me. Hmm. I guess I see things through Rosie-colored glasses."

Her lips twitched like she wanted to smile. "Corny. But cute. I guess I do the same, except I start out with low expectations for most people. It saves a lot of time and energy."

He lingered while she double-checked the lock and then walked beside her across the parking lot. "You deserve better. I'll wait for you while you take care of the gate."

A nod was all the acknowledgment she gave him, so he tugged on his helmet and climbed on his bike. Stray snowflakes drifted downward around him as he donned his gloves. The ride promised to be another cold one.

Fifteen minutes later, he stood in her kitchen, peeling off the heavy jacket, hooded sweatshirt, and flannel shirt that had kept him warm all day. He didn't need them anymore, not when she did the same a few feet away. Even the long-sleeved tee seemed unnecessary.

Her phone rang when she grasped his hand and led him toward the living room. She tossed the drugstore bag on the couch. Then she plopped down beside it, leaning into the corner of the plush cushions. "Crap! It's Thursday, isn't it? I forgot one of my clients had to reschedule. Have a seat while I take this call."

A tiny pang of jealousy hit, but he stomped on it and sat in the recliner on the other side of the corner table. She was trying to make ends meet, and he had no right to begrudge her that. Hell, her hot talk had turned him on in a big way the evening of his interview. Who was he to complain?

After a friendly greeting, she lowered her husky voice, its roughness moving over his skin like the firm but gentle strokes of her hand on his naked body too many nights ago. Kindness mixed with sexiness, amplifying the feelings he had no control over. He could easily fall in love with her—if he hadn't already.

She glanced toward him and her cheeks flushed light pink. "You know I'm always ready for you. Undress me so you can taste and touch me."

He hesitated only a second before making the decision to accept the invitation she may or may not have intended for him.

Her mouth hitched upward on one side when he dropped to his knees and unfastened the button near the slight indentation of her belly button. "Yes, all the way off."

He wasted no time unzipping and stripping off her jeans. Her underwear slipped away with the outer layer, revealing her soft curves and the triangle of dark curls at the apex of her thighs. His cock twitched, but he moved on to the Bell Lumber button-down shirt and then to the T-shirt beneath.

She gasped when he brushed his thumbs across her taut nipples through her last remaining item of clothing. "Mmm. Take off my bra too. I want to be naked."

Following her instructions, he unhooked the fasteners at her spine and slid the straps from her faintly tanned shoulders. The cups fell away, leaving her breasts ready for feasting, but he kissed a path through the valley between them, lightly brushing his beard closer and closer to the tight buds. Her soft hums continued as he nibbled his way past her ribs and the faint lines crisscrossing her abdomen, a testament to her strength.

A sexy squeak accompanied his slow lick through her slick folds, and her breath hitched. "Go down on me. Taste me. Yes, just like that. Does it make your cock hard?"

A pressure-treated four-by-four fencepost had nothing on his dick.

He held her glassy-eyed gaze and nodded, but he didn't

speak. Instead, he smiled around her clit while he savored her salty-sweetness and cupped her breasts in his palms.

She arched into his hands, her breathing fast and shallow. "My nipples. I want you to touch them while you lick me. Make me come."

Again, he did as she told him, her body trembling with each flick of his tongue and strum of his fingers.

"Oh, God. I'm so close." Her thighs tightened around his head as she bowed off the couch and cried out.

He pulled her swollen clit between his teeth and sucked, drawing out the keening that filled the room and the tremors that shook her muscles.

She finally collapsed into the cushions, a dazed expression on her beautiful face. "Wow. That was amazing. You're welcome. Have a wonderful night."

Pushing to his feet required a bit of careful maneuvering to keep from pinching his dick in the snug crotch of his jeans, but he managed to stand and unzip without damage. He grinned down at her, the taste of her still in his mouth. "I love giving you orgasms. Want another one?"

She set aside her phone, tore open the box of condoms, and handed him a strip of six. Her satisfied smile made his insides quiver. "What do you think? Suit up so I can ride you like a biker chick."

"You'd look hot in black leather. Almost as hot as you are naked." He shoved his pants past his knees, sat bare-assed next to her, suited up, and lifted her onto his lap. His mind nearly snapped when she lowered herself onto his hard-as-nails erection. The feel of her body wrapped around him took his breath away. "Damn. I've been thinking about you like this all day, every day since Tuesday."

Her fingers slid into his hair and she rocked forward and

back. “Me too, but I wasn’t expecting you to get me off while I talked to a client. Kinky, are you?”

“Better by me than the guy who called.” He hugged her against him and kissed the buzz-cut side of her head. “I want you all to myself, even if you decide to use those fuzzy handcuffs in your nightstand drawer on me.”

“Good, because I don’t want to share you, either.” She guided his lips to hers, nipping and then easing her tongue inside for a long and slow kiss that matched the rhythm of their bodies.

Each smooth stroke heightened his pleasure, joining with her as close to heaven as he’d ever been. Nothing in his life had ever felt more right, more perfect.

She moved slow and steady for what seemed like forever and no time at all, until all he wanted was to sweep her away with him into pure bliss. Her muscles shook and she moved his hands from her waist to her ass. “Help me make you come.”

Guiding her toward him, he rose up to meet her. The motion drove him balls-deep, a sensation that nearly stole his control. “Come with me.”

With the next rough thrust, she threw her head back and gasped, urging him past the point of no return. Their cries broke the relative quiet as light exploded behind his eyelids and heat rushed up his length. She collapsed into his arms, the place he wanted her to be for the rest of their lives.

I love you, Rosie.

The faint pings of knocking on glass cut through the sound of their uneven breathing.

He opened his eyes and found himself looking at a grinning woman on the other side of the window next to the front door. She raised a grocery bag and waved.

They’d been caught again.

CHAPTER EIGHT

"ARE YOU AND ROSE...GETTING PERSONAL?"

Barton tried to keep his eyes focused on the menu and failed. His hard stare located its target across the table from him in The Ringer Saloon. Getting caught with his pants down by a friend of the woman he loved a second time hadn't been on his to-do list today, let alone having other people speculate, especially if they thought he was only interested in getting laid. Hell, he'd gone from long-haul driving to wanting a long-haul relationship in the space of about a week. "That's nobody's business but hers and mine."

Simon chuckled and grabbed the handle of his frosty mug. "I'm just wondering who gave you the hickey. It wasn't there when you were out at the site this afternoon. She seems like the logical assumption since you were headed back to the lumberyard. You know, I don't think I've had one of those since college."

"Geez." Barton raised his hand to his neck, not sure if he could tell where it was by touch.

"Left side. Right below your ear, at the edge of your beard." After another snicker, the builder took a slug of his on-tap draft. "I've known her since I worked construction for my dad. Thirteen, fourteen years? She hasn't dated since her divorce, as far as I know."

"I wouldn't know about that." Barton's fingertips found a slightly sensitive spot where Cortez had indicated. Had she meant to mark him? The possibility excited him more than it should. "What's this side gig you're wanting me to do?"

"I'd like your help with—"

"Sorry for the delay, gentlemen." A woman, not the one who'd delivered their drinks, stepped up to the table and pulled an iPad from her server's apron. "Hi, I'm Carnie. Mae had an emergency, so I'll be taking over for her until she gets back. Would you like to hear about our specials? Or are you ready to order?"

Simon cast a glance at Barton. "I'm ready. How about you?"

Setting his menu aside, Barton nodded. "I'll have the quarter-pound burger—medium-well—with the works, coleslaw, and French fries. Can I get barbecue sauce instead of ketchup for the fries?"

She tapped the screen several times. "Absolutely. And for you, sir?"

Simon laid his menu on top of Barton's. "Make it two. No onions. Ketchup for the fries. You're the new owner, aren't you?"

After a few more taps, she looked up. Her friendly expression had shifted toward caution, probably because guys either hit on her all the time or thought a woman shouldn't own a bar. "I am. Carnie Burke. I hope you like the changes to the place."

"Good to meet you, Carnie. Simon Cortez of Cortez Homebuilders. One of my crew leaders recommended checking out The Ringer since it changed ownership. Good food and good service. And this Barton Holloway, a business associate."

"Thank your friend for the rec." Her near eye-roll said she wasn't impressed by his spiel or she suspected his comment about the service had more to do with the wait staff than the bar's improvements. "I'll put this order right in. Should be ready in about ten minutes. Can I get anything else for you while you're waiting? Pretzels? Another beer?"

"I think we're good for now. Thanks." Cortez adjusted his mug on the paper napkin until she walked away and then turned his attention back to Barton. "As I was saying, I'd like your help with a project."

"I CAN NAME THAT TUNE IN TWO SECONDS." POPPY CROSSED her ankles on the footrest of the recliner and dunked a pretzel in the mound of guacamole on her plate, looking way too smug.

Tapping the Play icon on her phone's screen, Rose shrugged. After a brief stint of Celtic fiddles, she tapped the Stop button and flipped over the timer. No way in hell would Poppy guess this one-hit wonder from 1982. "Name that tune."

Her friend narrowed her eyes and scrunched up her mouth. The pile of sand in the bottom of the hourglass barely formed a tiny hill before she lifted the pretzel to her mouth. "Dexy's Midnight Runners. 'Come On Eileen.'"

Sienna shook her head and flopped onto her back on the living room rug. "There's something seriously weird about your brain, Poppyseed."

Sitting cross-legged at the coffee table, Scarlet raised her phone, her wide grin suggesting she thought she had a shot at stumping the master. “My turn. We’re going back to the 70s. International boy band.”

Poppy’s patronizing smile was still as annoying as it had been for the past half hour. “I can name that tune in…three seconds.”

Electric guitars strummed for one long beat and then four quick ones before the opening cut off.

Rose pressed her lips together to keep the answer locked inside—because her dad had played AC/DC every day of her childhood. She’d been able to recite the lyrics to all their songs by fifth grade, much to the chagrin of her mother.

Scarlet’s fingertips drummed on the table. “Tick-tock, tick-tock.”

Her eyebrows dipping into a low vee, Poppy frowned. “AC/DC.”

“And the song title?”

The doorbell rang, and Rose popped up from her spot on the couch to answer the front door. “That’s probably Carnie.”

Cerise tagged along behind her. “Should be. I just got a text from her that she’s here.”

A peek through the window confirmed their guest had arrived, and a blast of cold air swirled around Rose as she let her inside. “Glad you could make it, Carnie. Come on in. I’m Rose. I had to leave the Halloween party early, so it’s good to finally meet you.”

The woman tugged her hat off, revealing a head of auburn hair several shades darker than Poppy’s—nothing like Bo Peep’s blonde ringlets from the gathering at the saloon. “Hi, Rose. It’s nice to meet you too. Cerise, good to see you again. Sorry I’m late.”

“No worries.” Rose took her hat and then her coat. “Such is the life of a small business owner. Help yourself to food and have a seat anywhere. What can I get you to drink?”

After they'd settled around the coffee table a few minutes later and shared more hellos, Scarlet nudged Poppy's foot. "Okay, time was up five minutes ago. Name that tune."

The know-it-all look was gone from their friend's face. "It isn't 'Dirty Deeds' or 'TNT.' 'Rock and Roll Ain't Noise Pollution' maybe?"

"Nope. I win!" Scarlet winked in Rose's direction. "Thanks to our hostess with the mostest for inspiring my song choice."

"Why? What was it?" Poppy glanced back and forth between them.

The gleam in Scarlet's eyes warned Rose to take cover. "I got here a little early, like five forty-ish, and what did I spy on the couch through the window? Rosie riding her new delivery man to the big O. I think 'Big Balls' was an appropriate choice. He's got an impressive pair on him."

Grabbing the pillow beside her, Rose buried her face in it as raucous laughter surrounded her.

"You had sex with Barton again?" Sienna fired the question and didn't even take a breath. "How long have you been getting naked with him? And why didn't you tell us it was more than a one-time thing?"

Cerise's amused voice broke through the chaos. "Since at least Monday when I dropped off her Pleasure Palace order and a minimum of twice, based on eye-witness accounts."

"Barton? Barton Holloway?"

Was that Carnie talking? A tiny peek confirmed it.

"I met him at the bar earlier. He was having dinner with a guy named Simon Cortez. They were talking about you."

"Me?" Rose lowered the pillow and discovered five sets of eyes watching her. "I've never even kissed Simon, let alone slept with him, so they couldn't have been comparing notes. Why would they be talking about me?"

Carnie balanced a plate on her lap with her knees pressed together, looking far too ladylike to own a small-town bar. "I only caught bits and pieces of their conversation while I was taking their orders and delivering their food and refills. Barton asked what the side gig was, and Simon—who seems to think he's God's gift to women, the big flirt—wanted help with a project. Then they were talking about you and Bell Lumber and how an influx of cash could expand your business. I don't normally eavesdrop on people's private discussions, but your name came up and… Anyway, Barton didn't say anything about the two of you doing the horizontal mambo."

Scarlet barked a laugh. "Oh, they weren't horizontal. He was sitting right there where Rose is now and she was straddling his lap."

Fighting another wave of embarrassment, Rose shook her head. "Says the woman who had sex on her kitchen counter with a total stranger who also happens to be my daughter's best friend's father."

"It was mostly on the stool by the breakfast bar. Also not horizontal." Her friend wore a smirk, probably the same one she'd worn when she propositioned Nelson. "Besides, what else is a horny woman supposed to do when a man checks out her naked body parts on her front porch?"

Carnie's eyes widened and she set her enchilada-loaded fork on her plate. "You answered the door naked? I want to hear this story."

Looking quite proud of herself, Scarlet stretched out on the rug near Sienna. "It's more complicated than a simple yes or no. A little context. Menopause makes me want sex all the time. I know, I know. There're worse things in the world, but my vibrator wasn't doing the job. During one of our get-togethers last spring, Rose and Cerise challenged me to have sex with the first eligible bachelor I met to help alleviate the problem. I accepted the challenge, completely unaware that my robe would fly open when I chased my parents' dog out the front door, flashing my fiancé the first time we met. It all worked out. He was only a tiny bit hesitant when I propositioned him."

"Nelson, right? Batman at the Halloween party?" Carnie seemed far too excited about the details. "I never would've guessed he was that kind of guy. He seems so quiet."

"He's a little shy, but the man growls when we're alone."

A loud snort came from Poppy. "Like we all needed to know the sex sounds he makes. Next thing you're going to tell us is Barton groans, because I want that in my brain every time I see him."

Cerise refilled her wineglass at the makeshift drink station on the end table. "Barton bellows. It's actually pretty impressive. Reminds me of King Kong or Sasquatch."

In dire need of an escape and a triple-fudge brownie, Rose grabbed her empty plate and pushed to her feet. "Better than a grunter who only gets himself off. Want me to grab you some dessert before it's gone, Carnie?"

"I'll come with you." Carnie shoveled in another bite of enchilada and moved her plate from her lap to the coffee table.

Fairly certain her nod meant she was ready, Rose led the newest addition to their group into the kitchen. "Sienna brought brownies, I picked up a coffeecake from the bakery, and Scarlet brought lemon bars. Nelson made them, so they're safe to eat."

"Ooh, my favorite. My grandma made them all the time when I was a kid." Plate in hand, Carnie added two lemon bars and then a brownie and a narrow wedge of coffeecake. "My boys love them too."

"You have kids? How old are they?" Two brownies from the center of the pan called Rose's name.

"Twenty-five and twenty-three. Do you have any other children besides the daughter whose best friend's father is Nelson?"

Rose pointed to a picture on the fridge from Meg's graduation party. "A son, Beau. He's twenty. Meg'll be nineteen next month. What made you decide to buy The Ringer?"

A look of pure satisfaction spread across Carnie's face. "I got it as part of my divorce, but I agreed to let my ex continue managing it if he made it profitable within a year. I fired him two months ago and started making changes."

"That must've been satisfying. And you're making a profit already, right?"

"Very satisfying since he met his barely legal girlfriend there. We're officially in the black as of four o'clock this afternoon, so I gave myself a few hours off to celebrate—after my best server got back from taking care of a family emergency." Carnie added a third lemon bar to her hoard. "Speaking of celebrating, Barton and Simon seemed to strike a deal tonight. A handshake and everything."

"As long as it doesn't interfere with his hours at the lumberyard, I'm okay with him making some extra money on the side. We all have bills to pay." After more than a decade of running a Hot Talk line, Rose could hardly throw stones. Leading the way back to the living room, she sighed at the current conversation related to the toy Cerise had dropped off Monday evening. "No, I haven't had the chance to try out the BOB-arian, with or without a partner."

"Ooh, what's this barbarian thing you're talking about?" With a lemon bar at the ready, Carnie returned to her spot on the couch. "Something from your toy store, Cerise?"

Glad for the redirection, Rose joined her new friend and

savored a big bite of brownie. Her thoughts wandered while Cerise described Conan and several other popular vibrators. None of them could possibly compare to Barton. Despite his bad luck with marriage, the man knew exactly what to do with his mouth and his cock. In fact, feigning exhaustion so her friends would clear out and she could catch him before he headed home crossed her mind. Spending another entire night with him in her bed sounded like the perfect way to end her day.

Her phone buzzed against her hip, interrupting her wishful thinking. A quick peek at the sender made her heart beat a little stronger and a little faster. Barton's text shouldn't make her feel like swooning. Wasn't she too old for that?

"Hope you're enjoying the time with your friends. Miss you already. Can't wait to see you tomorrow." A single red heart popped up a second later.

She sighed and tapped in a return message. *"Having fun. Miss you too. I think I'm falling in love with you."* How had that happened? Too chicken to say the words, she deleted the last sentence and sent the text. Then she added a smiling kiss face.

Giggles erupted around her as she put her cell face-down on her thigh.

Scarlet made smoochy noises. "Lover boy's texting you, isn't he? Did you tell him you're in love with him yet?"

An automatic denial broke from Rose's mouth before she considered her present company. "Who said—"

"Spare us the bullshit." Poppy waved her hand. "Sienna and I could see it written in your starry-eyed gaze when he walked in the office earlier. Rosie and Barton sitting in a tree, F-U-C-K-I-N-G. First comes Rose. Second comes Barton. They need more condoms in a jumbo carton."

Rose tried and failed to hide a grin while she typed in

another text. *"Any chance you're still in town? Stay the night with me?"*

His answer popped up almost immediately. *"Be there in ten minutes."*

As ready as she ever would be for a serious relationship, she pushed to her feet. "I guess that means you won't mind if I tell you to leave because my boyfriend is on his way over."

CHAPTER NINE

SLOWLY EASING AWAY FROM THE EDGE OF SLEEP, ROSE rolled over and wallowed in the satisfying twinge in her muscles. An arm draped across her waist and tugged her against the solid body next to hers, cocooning her in warmth. She opened her eyes, wanting to watch Barton sleep in the filtered rays from the outside security light, but his gaze met hers with the first blink.

His lips curved upward. "Good morning."

"G'morning." Yes, it was a very good morning. For the first time since her mid-twenties, romantic love flowed through her veins, giving her hope that she wouldn't spend the rest of her life alone.

"I love waking up next to you." He kissed her forehead and then pulled back far enough to caress her cheek. "I love you."

Elation surged through her, drowning a tiny spark of fear. Hearing the words again wasn't scary, like she'd always assumed it would be. He'd given her no reason to doubt his declaration and every reason to trust him. How was she supposed to resist this sweet and kind man?

She placed her hand over his heart, pretty sure its rhythm matched her own. "I love you too."

The happiness in his eyes offered a glimpse at how much her response pleased him. "I've waited a long time to hear that, and it's better than my fourteen-year-old self ever dreamed."

Her pulse skipped and hopped at that knowledge. "So it was worth the wait?"

"Definitely."

"I'm glad." Her lucky stars deserved a huge thank-you for bringing him back into her life. "If you grab a condom and take a shower with me, I'll blow the mind of your inner fourteen-year-old."

His low rumbling chuckle vibrated the bed. "You've already done that several times, but he's willing to oblige you again."

"I bet he is." She waggled her eyebrows at him and pressed her lips to his for a quick kiss. "Give me two minutes, young man."

"Yes, ma'am." He helped her slip out from under the covers, but the heat of his stare followed her all the way to the bathroom. "I'm counting the seconds."

"Me too." Casting a backward glance over her shoulder, she eased the door closed and leaned against it. Falling in love at fifty left her giddier than dating bad-boy Todd, who'd tricked her foolish hormones into thinking he actually cared about her at twenty-eight. Hell, the guy she'd gone to the homecoming dance with and let touch her boobs at eighteen hadn't inspired feelings like this.

She cracked open the door at the count of one hundred twelve with steam rising toward the exhaust fan.

Barton's footsteps announced his presence in the bathroom before he joined her. He set the foil packet on the toiletry shelf and stepped in, offering her a hand when she followed. The look of utter contentment on his face made her adore him even more. “Do you think anybody’ll catch us having sex this time?”

She hooked her arms around his neck and pulled him flush with her body. Every nerve ending went on full alert, raring to go another round with her amazing lover. “Nobody better be barging into my house at five in the morning unless there’s a fire or somebody died.”

“They can wait.” His mouth descended to hers, first with light brushes of his soft lips and then lingering tastes as his tongue slow-danced in a way that soothed and excited her. He backed her under the spray, still kissing her like he needed the physical contact to survive. His fingertips skimmed along her skin with the water droplets and triggered the same need in her. When he broke the connection, his panting breaths tickled her ear. “I wish I had time to kiss and touch you everywhere.”

She moved his hand from her right hip to her right breast before cupping his balls. Scarlet’s song choice for Poppy had been right on the money. “The feeling’s mutual.”

Not waiting for more direction, he adjusted the showerhead, sat on the built-in seat at the edge of the spray, and grabbed the condom packet. “Want to put it on me? I need to be ready so you can ride me after I go down on you.”

The position that provided her with the most pleasure had obviously become a favorite of his as well.

She knelt in front of him, taking a few moments to lick the swollen vein running up the length of his thick erection and to lap the bead of fluid from the head. Water sluiced down her back and fell from her hair to his strong thighs as she rolled the protection into place. The hitch in his breath and his soft groan urged her to stroke him one more time and suck the drip from his pert nipple.

"My turn." His gruff tone sparked a contraction low in her belly. "Stand up. I'll make sure you don't fall."

She'd already fallen for him, hard and fast, but he'd caught her and made her feel safe and loved. She pushed aside the what-ifs that tried to surface, ready to focus on the here and now—and their future together. For the first time in forever, she could envision a future with a man, imagine sharing her nights with someone who truly cared about her happiness.

"Are you okay?" The concern in his eyes enveloped her in a soft blanket. "Let me help you up."

He grasped her waist and lifted her to her feet in an easy motion before she could answer.

She cradled his jaw in her palms and put all the good feelings strumming through her soul into a kiss. It was sweet and sensual, urgent and thorough, everything she felt for him. She came up for a breath and rested her forehead on his. "I'm more than okay. Love me."

"In every way." He guided her leg over his shoulder, putting his mouth inches from the part of her aching for his touch. Then he parted her with his tongue and swiped through her folds in a long, slow lick. His worshipping gaze locked on hers as he flicked and sucked her clit.

Tingles rushed along her skin, her knees threatening to give out, but his arm around her waist steadied her as he worked his magic. She threaded her fingers into his hair and let the sensations carry her toward the heavenly place she always found with him.

One of his hands tightened around her hip and the other smoothed over her ribs and up to her breast. His thumb and finger rolled her nipple back and forth, adding to the building pleasure.

He released her clit, bringing a second of frustration, before he sent a puff of warm breath flowing over her. “Mm, you taste so good.”

A whimper tried to climb from her throat, but it became a relieved cry when his lips closed over the sensitive bud again and drew her past the edge into oblivion. Her legs trembled as wave after orgasmic wave threatened to drown her. She clutched at his arms to keep from slipping away with the water and floating upward with the steam.

Then she was on his lap, her body connected to his for another upward climb. He rocked into her in time with their ragged breaths and urgent mating of their tongues. His desperate groans and every erratic thrust of his cock carried her higher until she shattered into a million pieces. He shuddered and let loose a roar that promised he’d reached the same heights.

Gathering her even closer, he held her until her heart slowed to its normal rhythm and his rough panting changed to easy breaths. “This is where I belong. Right here with you. From now on.”

She couldn’t disagree. They’d both earned a relationship with love and trust and respect. They’d earned the right to be happy. This leap didn’t require faith. She could depend on him, and he’d proven himself worthy. “I want you to move into the house instead of the garage apartment.”

“SEE YOU IN THE MORNING, ROSE.”

She waved through her office door at the guys who

worked the service counter and closed her laptop. "Have a good night."

Their voices and footsteps faded before she found the energy to push to her feet. No sooner had she grabbed her coat and pulled the door closed, Barton walked in the side entrance, looking as delicious as a hot toddy on a cold day in his work clothes and boots.

He held up the keys and greeted her with a smile, the same friendly but professional one he used any time they crossed paths at the lumberyard. "You look tired. Want me to lock the front door and take care of the keys?"

She had no idea how he managed to keep their relationship under wraps, even if she appreciated the why of it. God only knew she couldn't help wanting to jump his bones whenever they were in the same room. Her phone buzzed against her hip as she opened her mouth. She reached for her pocket, not sure who would be calling until her hand closed around her cell. "Oh, it's Monday, isn't it?"

"Yep."

"Meg calls me on Mondays at closing time." Her stomach somersaulted at the realization she needed to tell her kids she was shacking up with her deliveryman. "I'll get the keys if you lock the door."

"Talk to your daughter. I can do both." Long strides carried him toward the main entrance as she tapped the Answer button.

She lifted the phone to her ear. "Hey, Meg. How's school?"

"Hi, Mom. I'm ready for Thanksgiving break, but school's good. You're making a big turkey like last year, aren't you? Did you invite Em and Ry and their dad? And Scarlet, of course. What about Mr. and Mrs. Brinks?"

The chatter about next week's holiday eased some of

Rose's nervousness, even though she couldn't begin to guess what Meg's reaction would be. "Yes, I invited the Whitakers and Scarlet and her parents."

"I think I'll make a peach pie and a pumpkin pie this year instead of two pumpkin. And don't forget the whipped cream."

"Already on the list." Barton's approach reignited the nerves, but Rose gestured toward the exit, determined not to put off the news. "I have something I need to tell you. Can you do a three-way call so I can talk to you and Beau at the same time?"

"Are you sick? Is it serious?" Panic laced her daughter's words.

"No, I promise it's nothing like that." Rose followed Barton outside and dug in her jeans pocket for her keys. "Get your brother on the call while I lock the door and the gate."

"Okay. Hold on."

When she climbed back in the truck after securing the gate, she switched to speaker and set her phone in the cupholder. Barton's hand closed around hers and squeezed, like he understood the potential freak-out she might have to deal with—her children's and possibly her own.

"Mom? Are you still there? Pull over. We're FaceTime-ing."

"Okay. Give me a sec." She left the truck idling and closed her eyes through a calming breath. Again, Barton's gentle touch grounded her. She picked up her cell, tapped the button to connect, and schooled her expression, as ready as she'd ever be for a face-to-face chat with Beau and Meg about her love life. "Hey, Beau. How'd you manage to find five minutes this time of day?"

Her son frowned. "I always have time to talk to you. Besides, Meg says something's wrong. Is Todd—"

"No." She tried not to roll her eyes at the automatic assumption. "It doesn't have anything to do with your father. I'm…dating someone."

A full minute of silence filled the cab before Beau grunted. "Who is he? It isn't Simon Cortez, is it? I don't trust him."

The eye-roll won. "Cortez Homebuilders is Bell Lumber's best customer. But, no, not Simon. I hired a new delivery driver. Barton Holloway. We went to high school together and things just sort of clicked."

Meg squealed and clapped her hands. "That's awesome! Were you like a couple? And now you're back together?"

A snuffle came from Barton's direction, and a glance at him revealed a man about to bust at the seams as he clearly tried not to laugh out loud.

Rose pressed her lips together and prayed for her self-control. "He asked me to a dance and I said no because I thought he was too young. I was a senior and he was a freshman."

Meg's smile lit up her face. "That's so cute! Do you like him a lot?"

Beau shook his head. "So, how serious are you about this guy? What did he do before you hired him? Has he been married before? Is he widowed? Is he divorced? Why did he get divorced? Does he have kids?"

Annoyance surged through Rose's body, but she refrained from addressing her older child by his full name. "Serious enough to tell you about him. He's sitting right here next to me if you'd like to ask him those questions directly. Barton, say hello to my nosy and over-protective son."

Barton finally exploded with a bellowing laugh as she aimed her phone at him. He slipped it from her fingers and faced his inquisitor with a relaxed grin. "Good to meet you,

Beau. Meg, it's a pleasure. Your mom talks a lot about both of you. I'm a former long-haul truck driver. Married twice. Divorced twice. Was cheated on both times. No kids. And I'm madly in love with your mother. I can't speak for her, but I'm thinking it might be a little too soon for a marriage proposal, so we're living together for now."

"*Living together?*" The disbelief in Beau's tone suggested his chin had hit the floor and his eyes had practically bugged out—like when he was five years old and she informed him listening to the radio while a spider bit him wouldn't turn him into Spiderman. "How long has this been going on?"

Tilting her cell until she could see his face, Rose aimed a death-stare at her son. "First of all, who's the parent? Second of all, that's our business, not yours. And third, your behavior means I get to grill anyone you introduce to me, including asking about previous relationships, sex, marriage—"

"Okay, okay. I'm sorry. It's just that I don't want another loser like Dad taking advantage of you." Beau's sigh signaled her to turn the screen back toward Barton. "And I'm sorry for giving you the third degree, Mr. Holloway."

"Call me, Barton. Apology accepted. I'm glad you're looking out for your mom. She's a special lady." He leaned across the console and kissed her cheek. The light brush of his beard on her skin triggered a warm shiver straight to her lower belly.

Despite the distraction, she forced her attention to her kids. "We're heading home now. Everything settled?" Their synchronized nods brought relief. "Talk to you soon. Love you both bunches."

"Love you too, Mom." Beau's gaze swung toward Barton. "So, I guess we'll see you next week for Thanksgiving."

Barton nodded. "I'm looking forward to it."

As soon as her son dropped from the call, Meg huffed a

noisy sigh. "Don't worry about Bo-Bo. He'll get used to the idea. Love you, Mommy. Nice to meet you, Barton."

Not surprised by her kids' night-and-day reactions, Rose disconnected and leaned back in the driver's seat. "Well, that was fun. What do you say we go home and talk about the marriage proposal?"

CHAPTER TEN

"HOLLOWAY, YOU GOT A FEW MINUTES?" CLAD IN A BUSINESS suit and hardhat, Cortez waved him toward the site office.

"Yep." Barton set the last bucket of nails on the ground for today's two-man crew of unloaders and crossed to the trailer. "What can I do for you, Simon?"

"Let's go inside." The builder led him into the single-wide mobile home and past a tiny kitchen to a miniscule office with a narrow table and a pair of metal folding chairs, not what he expected at all. Calling it sparce would be generous. "Have a seat. I want to go over the plan for next week. You're available Monday through Thursday, right?"

Pulling off his work gloves, Barton nodded. "As long as the moving truck's ready to go, I can bring a load over to the model home at lunchtime and another after I drop off the Bell Lumber delivery truck right before closing time."

"Great. I'll make sure everything's set at the warehouse. One of the guys'll ride with you and run you back to the lumberyard. Don't want to piss off Rose by making you late for your next delivery. I think she's still holding a grudge from my offer to buy into the business." The chair creaked as Simon rested his elbows on the edge of the table. His expression sparked a gut-deep warning that unsettled Barton's stomach. "I also overheard a conversation this morning you might be interested in since you're living with her. And before you ask how I know about that, small-town gossip is alive and well in Bell. I heard a cashier and a customer talking about it in the grocery store over the weekend. No judgment, but I'm wondering how serious it is that you moved in with her already."

Barton stretched his legs out in front of him and crossed his ankles, weighing the man's intentions. "We've discussed marriage and it's a possibility way down the road. No rush, though. Right now, we're good with the ways things are. I told you I'm not going to try to influence her into accepting your investment in Bell Lumber. It's her decision. Period."

Cortez's chuckle said he saw more than Barton had intended to share. "Believe me, I got the message loud and clear from her. No, this is about her ex-husband. He's been in physical therapy at a medical rehabilitation facility and they're releasing him today. He asked her for a place to stay."

"Son of a dick. Gotta go." His insides tangling in knots, Barton scrambled to his feet and headed out of the trailer. Todd Chambers had sucked her dry for years, using their kids to wheedle one favor after another out of her while she worked her ass off to provide for her family. The man needed to get the hell out of her life for good.

He thumped his fist against the driver's door and climbed into the truck. His frustration couldn't begin to compare to hers, but she shouldn't put up with her ex's crap on the off-chance the leech might pay her someday.

His mood darkened with every mile of the drive to the

lumberyard. As much as he respected her decision to stay in contact with her ex, allowing the jerk to manipulate her into taking responsibility for his actions made no sense. She was strong and independent, self-reliant and smart. That she still possessed any kindness in her heart was a miracle.

He stalked into the building at almost ten minutes past five, not sure what to say when she confided in him. She'd undoubtedly offered Todd the garage apartment or the couch until he could manage on his own, not that the man seemed capable under the best circumstances.

Her door was closed and low voices carried from the office. The words jumbled together, too indistinct to understand.

He logged the repair he'd made to the forklift after lunch and stowed the equipment keys to kill time. Another full minute passed before the door opened and she appeared in the doorway, shoving an arm into her coat sleeve as she exited.

Her gaze caught his for a second before she glanced away and locked up. "Oh, you're here. I was just about to check to see if you were back yet. Ready to go?"

"Yeah." He followed the same routine they'd fallen into since his first day—waiting while she secured her office, the side entrance, and the gate. Tension, however, filled the cab of her pickup today. Or maybe it all belonged to him. Knowing what he did made her silence harder to take. "Didn't see you much since this morning. Busy day?"

She gave a curt nod as she headed out of town.

The minimal response sparked memories of coming home from days on the road to a wife who acted like she hadn't even noticed he'd been gone. His stomach tightened, and he slowly exhaled to shake off the sickening sense of déjà vu. Rose wouldn't keep secrets from him.

Her fingers flexed on the steering wheel during the entire

drive, but she didn't speak until they walked in the house. "Supper smells good. It's nice not having to cook when I get home."

He reached for her coat as she shrugged out of it. "It's nice having a meal with the woman I love. Take your boots off and have a seat. I'll set the table and carry the crockpot over."

She grasped the front of his jacket and pulled him toward her. Then her lips pressed against his, relaxing the knots in his gut. "Thank you. I love you too."

"You're welcome." Savoring the heat surging through his body, he gathered her in his arms for more physical contact. God, he'd missed seeing her, talking to her, and holding her during their workday. His stomach growled, intruding on the moment. "Let's eat."

"Good plan." Her lopsided smile spread all the way to his heart. The tension seemed to leave her jaw, easing the lingering remnants of concern that she might not be happy with their arrangement.

After another quick kiss, he took off his coat and work boots and set to work serving the supper he'd helped her prepare in the slow cooker early that morning. Sharing the simple chore and taking care of her filled the empty places in his life he hadn't known were there.

He finally sat at the table and picked up his fork. "I was thinking we could—"

She jerked her head toward the window at what sounded like the heavy clunk of a car door, and the tension returned to her jaw in an instant. Then her chair screeched as she pushed away from the table. "Wait here while I see who's out there."

His heart dove to his stomach. "Are you expecting someone?"

Instead of answering, she hurried to the door they'd

entered not more than fifteen minutes ago, shoved her feet in her boots, and disappeared outside. Only muffled voices made their way through the narrow opening of the door she'd left ajar, but he could easily guess who the visitor was.

Abandoning his supper, he crossed to the sink to watch his relationship go up in smoke. A lanky man using a cane faced her. A suitcase sat in the driveway and the car that he'd evidently arrived in rolled toward the road.

Rose's lack of trust in him hurt Barton more than when both of his ex-wives had shown their true colors. Disappointment sliced through him, deep and painful. His feelings obviously came in second to the jerk she refused to cut loose.

He patted his pocket for his keys, his wallet, and his phone on the short trek to the shoe mat. Everything was present and accounted for as he stepped into his riding boots and zipped them on. Considering the dropping temperature, he layered his leather jacket over his sweatshirt and lined flannel coat.

Cold air filled his lungs with his first breath outside the house, and the conversation abruptly ended when the screen door banged shut. Tugging on his gloves and keeping his eyes on his destination, he aimed for the garage.

"Barton?" The surprise in Rose's voice tempted him to ask her why she hadn't told him about letting her ex stay with her. "Where—"

"I'm going for a ride." Not slowing, he focused on getting to his bike and putting on his helmet. One kick brought the engine to life, and he followed the lane to the road without looking back.

"DAMN IT, TODD, I TOLD YOU NO." THE LOW RUMBLE OF Barton's Harley faded, but Rose pinned her worst glare on her ex-husband for his unmitigated gall. Dealing with her lover's confusing behavior had to wait until the Todd-ler got his presumptuous ass off her property. "I don't care where you go. You're leaving or I'm calling the cops."

Todd leaned a little heavier on his cane and shot a familiar frown at her. "I guess you're not interested in getting the money I owe you. My lawyer says there's a very good chance he can win my personal injury case and that it's worth a lot of money."

"Bullshit." She crossed her arms in front of her chest, wishing she'd grabbed her coat on her way out of the house. "If you actually have a crackpot lawyer who thinks he can collect millions for you, go stay with him. I'm done saving your lazy ass. Now, leave."

His mouth opened and then closed, like he'd thought better of arguing with her. He dug a cell phone from his pants pocket, tapped at the screen, and lifted the device to his ear. "Hey, it's me. I need a ride."

She narrowed her eyes. If he could call someone for a ride that easily, why the hell couldn't he ask them for a place to stay?

Lowering the phone, he scowled at her. "Who's Barton? You got a boyfriend I don't know about?"

"None of your business." She tucked her fingers into her underarms instead of rubbing her hands against the cold.

"Is he living with you?" Todd shifted the cane in his grip and winced, but no sympathy came.

"None of your business."

"How long—"

She growled, hating every second she had to wait for her

stupid ex to leave. "I said it's none of your business, so shut your mouth and keep it shut."

His eyes widened. "What's gotten into—"

"Did I not just tell you to shut it?" A faint chirp tempted her to run inside to check her text messages, but she planted her feet, determined to make sure Todd actually left. "One more word. That's all it'll take to—"

Gravel crunched and headlights flashed through the trees. Relief mixed with uncertainty when a car instead of a classic Harley pulled in next to Todd. Despite struggling with his luggage, he managed to load it in the backseat and slide in next to it. Then the beat-up sedan maneuvered into what should've been an easy three-point turn but turned into five before it putted out the lane.

She waited until the tail lights disappeared to stalk inside and lock the door behind her. Hopefully, she'd seen the last of him, even if it meant never collecting the child support he owed her.

Her cell chimed again, urging her toward the table. Meg's name and message lit up the screen.

"Thanksgiving break!!! Bo-Bo just picked me up. He brought pizza!!! Home in about 4 hours!"

Rose shook off a stab of exasperation that Barton hadn't texted or called. *"Okay. :) Drive carefully."*

Without pausing to overthink her actions, she tapped on his contact, in spite of the fact that he was probably still riding and wouldn't answer. After several rings, his voicemail offered its spiel. "Barton, it's Rose. What's going on? You seemed mad about… Well, not mad exactly. More like upset about something. I'll reheat supper and we can talk about it."

She scraped both plates of chicken and vegetables into the crock and returned it to its base to kill time while he stopped to check his phone and then drove back. He couldn't have gone far in the ten minutes or so since he'd ridden off into the falling dusk.

A half hour passed while she sorted laundry, started a load in the washer, and cleared the junk from her email. Another twenty minutes ticked by as she cross-checked the list for Thanksgiving dinner with the supplies in the fridge and pantry. Then she sat on the couch, trying not to let her impatience and hunger morph into hangry-ness.

What the hell was taking him so long to come home?

Her phone pinged on the cushion beside her, making her pulse skip, but the name sent her hopes diving to the ground. As much as she adored her friends, she needed Barton to tell her he was on his way.

"Are you busy? Need a sounding board."

Although Poppy's text didn't sound urgent, Rose typed in the answer she'd want to hear. *"Come on over."*

"Thanks. Be there in five."

The mothering part of her kicked in, taking her to the kitchen to make tea and pull clean dishes from the cupboard. Somebody should eat the overcooked meal simmering in the slow cooker, especially when her stomach was ready to cannibalize itself. Maybe Barton would show up as they finished off what was supposed to have been his supper too.

Three raps on the door announced Poppy's arrival and triggered a change from concern to annoyance at his absence.

Working her jaw to release some of the tension, she welcomed her friend into her empty house. "Hey, what's up? You hungry? I haven't eaten yet."

Poppy kicked off her shoes and followed Rose to the kitchen counter. "Food sounds great. I barely had time for lunch and just finished with my last cleaning job. Where's Barton tonight? You guys have been attached at the hip and other parts since he moved in."

Huffing out a sigh, Rose handed Poppy a plate. "I don't know. He got pissy about something and went for a ride on his bike. That was over an hour ago."

"Wait a minute." Her friend froze with the serving spoon poised above the contents of the crockpot. "Barton's mad at you? What about? He practically worships you."

"I have no idea." The annoyance morphed into stinging eyes and a knot in her throat. By the time they sat at the table, Rose had her emotions under control again—at least to the extent that she wasn't on the verge of bawling. "Let's hash out your problems first."

"Simon Cortez asked if I was interested in bidding on a contract to clean all his new homes after their construction is complete." Poppy stuffed a forkful of potato into her mouth and chomped on it like a wad of Bubble Yum.

"It sounds like an awesome opportunity to grow your business. You can hire a few people and focus more on the management side. Isn't that what you planned when you started Clean As A Whistle?"

"Yeah, but…" Looking toward her plate, Poppy stabbed a piece of chicken hard enough that it fell into a shredded pile. "You're absolutely not allowed to tell anyone this. Ever. Promise?"

Rose nodded, not sure what could be such a terrible secret. "Sure."

After gnawing on her bottom lip, Poppy exhaled and met Rose's gaze. "So, um, I had a one-night stand with Simon about two years ago after a wedding reception we both went to. I mean, it was no big deal and it isn't awkward when we run into each other. We say hi. No weirdness or anything. It's just that working with him… I don't know."

Dumbfounded by her friend's admission, Rose leaned

back in her chair. “Wow. You know he’s a player, right, Poppyseed?”

“What’s wrong with enjoying sex and not wanting a relationship if you’re upfront about it? I slept with him for the same reasons he slept with me. Get laid. No attachments.” The fork clinked against the dish, sounding too much like a text alert. “Besides, the sex was pretty damn good and he didn’t complain about supplying condoms or wearing them.”

Rose moved her phone closer to the edge of the table and flipped it right side up. “But can you work with him? How often would you see him? Like every day, once a week, almost never? And is the growth of your business more important than being a little uncomfortable?”

“See? This is why you’re the best person to talk to about stuff like this. You always ask the right questions and never pass judgment.” Poppy picked up her glass and tapped it against Rose’s. “No man or the fact that I know what his dick looks and feels like is going to keep me from going after what I want. Now, tell me what’s going on with you and Barton.”

“I don’t know.” Despite a long look at the screen, Rose’s phone stayed dark. “Everything was fine when we got home from work. We sat down to eat, but Todd showed up, even though I told him he couldn’t stay here to finish recuperating. I went outside to tell him to get lost. Then Barton came out a minute or two later, headed straight for the garage, and left on his bike. Said he was going for a ride.”

Poppy scrunched up her mouth and aimed a disconcerting stare at Rose. “He knew you weren’t letting Todd stay, right? Or could he have thought you changed your mind?”

“There was nothing to tell. Todd called me at lunchtime and again at closing time to ask about staying here and I told him no. That was supposed to be the end of the story.”

“But you didn’t tell him what happened. What was he

supposed to think when your ex showed up? Especially since you said both his wives cheated on him."

"I didn't want him to—" She'd wanted to protect him, the same way she protected her kids, except he was a grown man who was capable of taking care of himself. "You're saying I suck at communication."

Pointing a chunk of carrot at her, Poppy nodded. "Yep, and you're going to have to do something about it or risk losing the best boyfriend you've ever had."

CHAPTER ELEVEN

Cradling her third cup of coffee, Rose inhaled and hoped the fragrant steam eased the burning sensation in her eyes and the achiness in her throat. For the first time in her life, she'd cried herself to sleep over a man.

Barton hadn't come home last night or this morning. He hadn't texted or called. The true test of how hurt he was from her lack of disclosure—assuming that was why he'd taken off—would be if he showed up for work. Until seven o'clock rolled around in eight minutes, she could only speculate and cross her fingers.

Her phone buzzed against her desk, bringing a mix of hope and trepidation with it. What if he wanted to know when he could pick up all his stuff from her house? What if he quit his delivery job at Bell Lumber? What if he didn't want her apology?

She sniffled and braved a peek at her cell. Ripping off the Band-Aid had always been more her style than avoidance, but the prospect of never seeing him again sparked soul-deep grief.

A short message vanished before she saw who it was from

or what it said. She tapped the screen, entered her passcode, and navigated to her messages before she lost her courage. Her daughter's name topped the list.

"Good morning, Mommy."

Another message popped up.

"Got up early to have breakfast with you, but you're already gone. I didn't hear Barton come in last night. Have you heard from him?"

Meg had done a good job of convincing her brother to give Barton a chance, but all that had gone down the drain when the man in question hadn't been present when her kids had arrived home for their Thanksgiving break. Beau had threatened to pack up everything in the house belonging to her missing boyfriend and dump it by the mailbox out at the road.

A gulp of caffeine washed down most of the lump still lingering halfway down her throat. *"No call. No text. Waiting to see if he comes to work."*

The dots signaling an in-progress text bounced twice before Meg's next message appeared. *"Are you okay?"*

"I'll be fine." She was always fine. She'd survived thirteen years as a parent with no one to count on but herself. That took more gumption than getting over a broken heart. Besides, what other choice did she have?

She pushed up from her chair, leaving her mug and her phone in the middle of her desk, and trudged to the side entrance. Her other two employees approached the door as she turned the deadbolt. After a half-assed wave, she headed for the front of the store, all too aware of the time and Barton's absence.

Headlights flashed through the glass as she opened her business for the day, but two trucks and a van pulled into the parking lot instead of a classic Harley with the owner of her heart straddling its engine. Tears prickled her eyes again, and she swiped at the drop that leaked out and raced down the side of her nose.

Keys jingled as she hurried toward the employee restroom. The temptation to look for Barton proved too strong to resist, but only her long-time employees stood at the counter where the equipment keys were stored.

The younger of the two men tucked a sheaf of papers onto a clipboard and glanced her direction. "Barton's got a delivery to Cortez first thing this morning. He asked me to grab the keys to the truck and the purchase order while he checks the tire pressure."

"Okay." Her voice cracked, along with her heart in several new places, but she forced her legs to carry her to her intended destination instead of detouring outside to confront the man she loved. If he'd wanted to see her, he would've come into the building. Besides, she hated letting anybody see her cry.

In the restroom, she braced her hands on the sink and tried to breathe through the pain zinging between her burning eyes and aching gut. A bad case of the stomach flu wreaked less havoc. It also went away after a few days, unlike the agony of losing the man she'd hoped to spend the rest of her life with. That pain would last for years—if it ever went away.

Knocking interrupted her unsuccessful attempt to prepare herself for the workday. "Rose, Abbott Construction's on the phone."

She flipped on the cold water and tore a section of paper towel from the roll. "I'll be right there."

Life went on, whether she wanted it to or not.

After a few splashes of cool water to clear the blotchiness from her cheeks, she dried her face and headed back to her office. She closed the door partway and then reopened it to hang her THAT TIME OF THE MONTH: DO NOT DISTURB sign, the one she usually reserved for payroll and profit-loss statement days, on the knob. A firm push with her hip made the door click shut.

❧

BETWEEN AVOIDING THE MAIN BUILDING AND ROSE'S TRUCK being gone from the parking lot most of the afternoon, Barton hadn't caught even a glimpse of her all day. The guys had warned him to steer clear because of the sign they'd seen on her door, but it was a lie. Her period wasn't due for another week or more, depending on what menopause decided to do to her body this month. If she didn't want to face him, all she had to do was give him his walking papers. Or she could've had somebody else deliver the news for her.

He trudged to the counter to find the next order, still unsure if he wanted to see her or not. Hell, the possibility of quitting a job he enjoyed sat in the back of his head, waiting for a sign. Sleeping without her last night had turned into not sleeping, and he'd spent a good part of the night staring at the ceiling. Even if she'd laid out strict ground rules and set an eviction date, she hadn't told him about her houseguest. That was the problem.

If he'd wanted a relationship with secrets and no communication, he could've stayed married to wife number one or wife number two.

Paperwork in hand for the final delivery of the day, he stalked back outside, turning up his collar against the late-November chill. The constant movement from loading helped warm his body until he climbed behind the wheel and blasted the heater. A quick check of the dash gauges triggered a groan. Stopping for a fill-up needed to happen sooner rather than later, so he set out for the gas station a few blocks from the lumberyard.

As he pulled in next to the only diesel pump, a man with a cane in his right hand and a twelve-pack of cheap beer in his left hobbled his way out of the convenience store. Without looking up, he stepped off the sidewalk.

Barton climbed out and focused on his task, hoping he didn't witness the oblivious guy getting run over by a car.

"Hey, I know you." The *thunk-shuffle-thunk* gave away the speaker's identity. Beer Guy stood on the opposite side of the pump, using it as a support. "What were you doing at Rose's house yesterday? Did you talk her out of letting me stay there?"

Barton's brain scrambled to process two pieces of information. This idiot was Rosie's ex-husband, Todd, and she'd refused his request for a place to crash last night.

Relief hit several seconds before guilt took over. Nonetheless, Barton aimed a frown at the worthless excuse of a father. "It was her decision. Maybe she decided she's done letting you take advantage of her kindness and generosity, especially after you skipped out on your responsibilities. She made sure the kids you helped bring into this world had food and clothes, even when it meant working two jobs."

"What do you know about it?" Chambers shook his head, as if he could shake off his failures. Then he turned and headed toward a car idling near the end of the tiny store.

"Everything she told me."

The loser didn't look back to acknowledge the words, but it was probably for the best. Barton didn't need anyone pointing out the fact that he'd left without giving her the benefit of the doubt.

She'd shared the important parts of her life with him.

She'd trusted him with those details, and he'd jumped ship because she hadn't told him about a non-issue. He had to trust her as much with his feelings as she had with hers.

The drive to West Farmington and back toward Bell let him stew enough to make some decisions about his life and his future with Rose. Gun-shy or not about marriage, he loved her. Growing old with her wasn't hard to imagine. Yet, her simple statement during the post-introduction-to-her-kids discussion on the topic—that their approval mattered to her—had started him rethinking his perception of happily-ever-after, but it hadn't gone far enough.

Keeping his house with the idea to rent it out was a backup plan, as was holding on to the money from the sale of his rig instead of buying a car. His assertion that a piece of paper didn't have to define their relationship gave him a ready escape hatch if her feelings for him changed. He was no better than her ex.

How could he expect her to trust him to be reliable and supportive when he had one foot halfway out the door all the time? She deserved someone who was fully committed to her and her happiness.

❧

ANOTHER MINUTE CLICKED BY ON ROSE'S LAPTOP, ADDING TO the already buzzing tension in her body. She pushed away from her desk and paced to the side entrance, but the delivery truck was missing from its parking spot. Barton's Harley still sat a few spaces down from her pickup.

She slid her phone from her pocket to check her messages, fingers crossed that a simple breakdown had caused his lateness. The clock changed to five thirty as she tapped in her passcode. No new texts waited for her, so she took a calming breath and opened the previous thread with Barton. "Just ask if there's a problem. It's a boss thing, not a personal relationship thing."

"Truck problems?"

As she read and reread the brief message she planned to send, deep rumbling vibrated the air and the floor. Then the truck in question rolled past, bringing an unexpected surge of feelings, mostly relief that nothing terrible had happened to the man she loved. Her equipment was replaceable, but he absolutely was not.

Eight minutes passed before he finally lumbered through the parking lot toward the place she waited on the inside of the glass. He tugged his Bell Lumber baseball cap from his head, raked his fingers through his messy hair, and repositioned the hat as he walked. When he looked up, his gaze met hers and his lips thinned to a barely visible line between his moustache and beard.

Her stomach in knots, she stepped back far enough to let him in the door. "You're later than usual. Did the truck break down? Or did you have trouble with the delivery?"

"Three deer ran across the road just outside of town. An SUV clipped one and hit a car coming the other direction. Blocked traffic both directions until the cops and a pair of tow trucks cleared the road. Only minor injuries, but a pregnant woman went into labor." He pulled the delivery truck keys from his coat pocket and set them on the counter. His noisy exhale seemed like a warning that neither of them would like what he had to say next. Even so, his whiskey-smooth voice raised delicious goose bumps on her skin. "I owe you an apology for yesterday. I shouldn't have—"

"You had every right to walk out. I should've told you Todd asked if he could stay at the house for a few days." She let a spark of hope grow. If it meant she ended up with a broken heart, she'd deal with it later. "I'm sorry if I gave you the impression that your opinion didn't matter. It does."

He blinked at her, his expression conveying confusion. "This is my fault. You're used to handling every situation yourself. You've never done anything to give me a reason not to trust you, and I shouldn't have judged you based on my ex-wives' behavior."

Fairly certain they'd survived the first bump in their relationship, she stepped closer and brushed her palm along his thick beard. Its chill seeped through her skin, but touching him was so worth having cold fingers. "I screwed up and you panicked. Totally understandable, given our pasts and how fast things have happened between us. Are we okay now? I miss you and I want you to come home."

"I missed you too." His arms closed around her, drawing her to his chest. "There's just one more issue we need to settle. I know I said we should take our time deciding whether we wanted to get married or not, but I changed my mind. I'm ready to go all in. I want that commitment. I want to be your husband."

Joy spreading through her heart, she raised her head to smile up at him. "Are you proposing to me?"

"I am." His immediate response, along with the adoration glowing in his eyes, assured her he meant what he said. "I love you, Rosie. Will you marry me?"

She touched her lips to his, happier than she would've thought possible. "Yes. Let's go celebrate in my office."

His brows furrowed. "Are you sure you don't want to wait until we get home? The desk is kind of small."

"Too many people at the house." She led him past the counter and through her open door. "Meg invited a friend over to help with Thanksgiving prep and Beau's been putting up Christmas lights today."

"Sounds like the perfect conditions for getting caught with our pants down again." He grasped her hips and tugged her against his erection. "Twice was enough."

Giving in to a groan, she wiggled closer. "Once was more than enough. I might have to rethink my aversion to dresses. I could have you inside me already if I was wearing one right now."

His breath warmed her neck as he unfastened her carpenter pants. "What if I like undressing you? Not to mention, your butt looks pretty damn amazing in jeans."

She shoved the denim past her hips and yanked her boots through the leg holes. The layer beneath was conveniently gone too. "Yours looks pretty damn amazing naked. Drop your drawers and put on a condom while I enjoy the scenery."

"Yes, ma'am." He tossed the condom from his wallet into the top tray of her organizer stand.

"Mom? Are you in here?"

She barely swallowed a squeak at Meg's voice. Panic sent her grabbing her pants from the floor, gesturing for Barton to reverse course, and then hurrying to sit behind the desk to hide her bare bottom and legs. "In the office."

Her daughter came into view a few seconds later—thankfully after he rezipped. She glanced at Rose, over toward Barton, and back again. "Hi, Mom. Barton. You're working things out, aren't you? You're adults. You can do this."

Rose picked up a pen to give her hands something to do. "We just finished talking. Everything's fine now. Great, in fact."

"Awesome. Beau, Em, and I are on our way to pick up pizza for supper, so I guess we'll see you at home in about ten minutes." Her gaze dipped toward the corner of the desk with the stacked trays for in-progress orders and paperwork to be filed. A dimple appeared in Meg's left cheek as her smile became a grin. "Well, unless you have other plans."

Barton's face flushed bright red and the choking sound he made gave away his intentions. "Twenty minutes. Maybe thirty."

With a wave, Meg spun around and headed out of the office. "Take your time. Oh, and you should probably lock the door behind me so you don't get interrupted again."

Giggles echoed through the high-ceilinged space long enough for her daughter to have reached the exit.

A full minute passed before Barton trailed after Meg. "I'll lock the door."

Rose sighed. God, he was so damn cute and sexy and chivalrous. How had she not seen those traits thirty-two years ago and saved them the trouble of three failed marriages?

He re-entered her office, turned the deadbolt, and crossed to where she sat. The bulge behind his zipper triggered a ripple of anticipatory joy through her body, but she didn't hurry him as he freed the lovable beast and rolled on the condom. Everything about this moment was too perfect to rush.

She stood, needing to touch and kiss him, to renew their connection in every way possible.

As their lips met, he lifted her off her feet and braced her back against the wall. "Wrap your legs around me and hold on tight."

His cock slipped inside her with the motion, filling her body the way he filled her heart. A feeling of rightness surged through her. "I'm never letting go. You're mine and I'm yours. Forever."

He smiled, all his love for her shining in his eyes. "And no more interruptions."

Are you ready for the next story in the Romancing the Phone series? Get *Hang-Ups*!

Thanks for reading! If you enjoyed this story, please consider leaving a review on the retailer's website, BookBub, and/or Goodreads to help other readers find their next book! Join my Facebook reader group for fun discussions and subscribe to my newsletter to receive the latest news about releases, sales, book signings, and more.

HANG-UPS SNEAK PEEK

Chapter 1

"RIGHT THERE. YOU NEED TO GO FASTER." A FEMININE groan came from somewhere near the checkout counter. "I can't hold this position much longer."

From his vantage point right inside the front entrance of BOB's Pleasure Palace, Dixon Mayhew could only use his imagination about what was going on between the woman and his most-experienced technician. He wanted sex as much as the next divorced middle-aged man, not that he got any, but doing it during an installation job—even in an adult toy store—violated his work policies. That his employee had a wife and kids while he was screwing around disgusted him even more. He wouldn't have pegged the guy for a cheater. "Rodney."

A clunk preceded another groan, this one obviously belonging to his tech. "Just a sec, boss. Got to make a quick adjustment."

Shaking his head, Dixon waited next to a display filled with every possible size, color, texture, and flavor of lubed and un-lubed condoms on the planet. A tall rack of furry handcuffs stood to the right of it and a shelf of neon orange, pink, and blue vibrators flanked it on the left. He was no prude, but…

A shiny chain caught the light, drawing his eyes to a wide padded band with a buckle at one end and a loop of the same material at the other.

Is that what I think it is?

A headful of silvery-blonde hair popped up beside the shoulder of a black leather bustier-clad mannequin with a spiked collar around her headless neck. Crotchless panties left the very nearly anatomically correct parts at the tops of its cut-off thighs uncovered. When the real woman turned toward him, his dick went from forty-four and mostly limp to eighteen and perpetually horny in less than two seconds.

A strapless Caribbean-aquamarine jumpsuit clung to every one of the bombshell's curves, suggesting beach weather instead of a brewing late-March snowstorm. She slipped her bare feet into feather-adorned heels that added at least three inches to her petite stature. Sexy pink-polished toes peeked out the front of the shoes.

God, the woman had it going on from head to toe.

Chill, dude. Seriously. She's someone's daughter, possibly sister, and maybe granddaughter. Just like Syd.

His daughter would smack him upside the skull for thinking with his other head—and she'd be justified, whether he was suffering from a ridiculously long dry spell or not.

His employee rose behind the counter and tucked a pair of needle-nosed pliers into his back pocket. "The wiring's in for the upgraded surveillance system. It took the two of us almost twenty minutes to thread the damn line past the— *Darn.*

Sorry about the cursing, ma'am. Anyway, it's ready to test the video feed."

They were feeding wires, not fucking each other's brains out. Get your brain out of the gutter.

She extended her hand toward Dixon as she crossed to him. "No worries, Rodney. My language is usually much more colorful. You must be Mr. Mayhew. I'm Cerise Wethers, the proprietor of BOB's Pleasure Palace. We spoke on the phone a few weeks ago."

Her professional manner seemed at odds with her husky voice and the sexpot persona she physically conveyed, not to mention the name of her adult toy store. Then again, why couldn't a woman exude confidence, intelligence, beauty, and loads of sex appeal all at the same time?

Closing his much-larger hand around hers, he kept his gaze locked on her face. Hopefully, his coat hid any evidence that he'd been looking elsewhere. "Ms. Wethers, it's good to finally meet you. Call me Dixon."

"Dixon." She nodded once, withdrew her hand, and set off at a brisk walk toward the rear of the shop. "Follow me. My office is in the back room. I really appreciate your willingness to complete the job while the shop is closed."

"I'll finish up here, Rodney. You can head out as soon as you're done loading up. Things are getting nasty out there." He trailed after her, his leisurely pace allowing him to keep up with her and focus on the conversation instead of her swaying hips. "Rod and I are both early risers, so it works well for us. With commercial projects, we prefer to install before or after business hours. When we work on the new system for your house, we'll shift to regular eight-to-five hours."

"Okay." Not slowing, she pushed through the wide employees-only door and veered to the right past three large unopened boxes. Then she flipped on the light switch as she entered a decent-sized space with a functional desk and a lavish seating area. “I take alternating Mondays and Tuesdays off. We can discuss how to handle the interior components after you’re finished testing everything here. Would you like a cup of coffee?”

“Yes, thank you. Black’s fine.” A quartet of screens hung on the wall across from the desk, drawing his attention.

“The Keurig and a selection of coffee and tea are on the sideboard. Mugs are there too. If you change your mind about sweetener or creamer, help yourself. Half-and-half is in the mini fridge.” After retrieving a clipboard and a laptop from the table between the couch and chairs, she headed toward the doorway. “I’ll be unpacking a shipment if you have any questions.”

Her casual do-it-yourself instructions annoyed him a little, but he had to admit he admired her polite refusal to play hostess when she had work to do. He did too, for that matter. “Thanks.”

A cloud of estrogen remained in the office long after she left him to check the hookups for the monitors and test the feeds to the cameras at the front and rear doors, at the cash register and strategic spots around the retail area, and in the stockroom and office. It left him antsy and wishing he didn’t need to inspect every completed job to satisfy his perfectionist gene. Even his high-maintenance ex-wife hadn’t drugged a room the way Cerise Wethers did.

A bark of feminine laughter carried from the stockroom into the office, and its owner held a pizza-sized box on the monitor across from where he sat at the desk. Her lips moved like she was talking to somebody, but the feed didn’t reveal anyone else in the wide-angle view. She added the box and several more of the same to the cart beside her. Then she tapped a key on the laptop and wrote what seemed to be a checkmark on the top paper of a clipboard.

Despite his curiosity about the item she'd unpacked, he downed another gulp of his coffee and went back to fiddling with the settings for the camera mounted at the customer entrance. After another failed attempt to bring the picture into focus, he headed back out to the sales floor.

His client looked up at him as he walked past her. "Done?"

He didn't slow, more to avoid an estrogen overdose than her question. "No. One of the cameras isn't working properly."

The click of her heels behind him suggested their conversation wasn't over. "Not the one at the checkout counter, I hope. That thing was a beast to wire."

"The front door." He continued through the stockroom and into the store. A near white-out greeted him on the other side of the glass. "I'm going out to my truck to get another camera. Be right back."

Flurries swirled around him on the short jog to the passenger side, making him wish winter had departed early from northeast Ohio. By the time he grabbed a spare from his emergency supply and ducked inside again, snow had managed to blow into his shirt collar and cling to his beard.

Cerise handed him a towel from under the checkout counter. "Looks wicked out there."

He swiped the cloth over his head and neck. "It is. Visibility is about ten feet and I'd guess there's almost an inch of snow already. Hard to tell with all the wind. It might be a good idea to close up and stay put when I'm done swapping out the units. Even if the road crews start now, they're not going to be able to keep up. Give me about five minutes to install the replacement."

The stubborn set of her jaw suggested she planned to argue the need to shut down her shop for the day, but she gave a firm nod and wiggled her ass through the stockroom door.

God, the woman exuded attitude, not unlike his daughter. Too bad he hadn't learned a damn thing from his weakness for self-confident women by marrying and divorcing one and raising another. Of course, Sydney didn't take pleasure in picking fights with him the way his ex-wife had. He'd done something right during Syd's teen years, despite Teri's never-ending criticism and interference.

The lights flickered twice as he positioned the stepstool beneath the malfunctioning camera. Only the bright snow outside kept him from abandoning the task until a day without a blizzard.

Brisk click-click-clicking approached from behind. "All the lights on the old security panel turned red and there's a lockdown message flashing in the armed and disarmed window. I'm fairly certain that's a bad thing."

"How the hell…" Abandoning the camera problem for the moment, he hurried to the main controls located near the delivery entrance in the back. One look at the control box confirmed that the system had gone haywire, most likely from the fluctuation in power and a bad connection.

"Do you know what's wrong with it?" Cerise's voice caressed his skin as if it were a living, breathing entity, triggering a mix of panic and instant hard-on.

Being trapped with the estrogen queen until the winter weather passed might bring an end to his monk-like existence, but he needed a girlfriend less than he needed a flat tire, a dead furnace, and a notification that his mortgage payment was late.

He punched in the access code and pressed the reboot

button. “The old system had some shorts in the wired elements and those may have experienced a power surge. There’s no way to override now, even though we’re almost ready to switch over to a wifi-based system with an all-new hardwired backup. We’ll try a restart and go from there.”

The lights flickered again, plunging them into pitch-black darkness.

Well, that didn’t go as planned.

The emergency light came on above the exterior door across the room, but it wasn’t near enough to do more than cast deep shadows throughout the stockroom.

Backlight outlining her curves in a perfect silhouette, Cerise pivoted away from him. “I have a flashlight in my office. Be right back.”

He nixed the idea to follow her the second it popped into his head, especially since the image that accompanied the thought put his hands on her shapely hips. What was wrong with his brain today? “Be careful. I still have a few tools on your desk.”

“Thanks for the warning.” She kicked off her heels at the doorway and tiptoed into the dark like a mischievous pixie. After several long moments and the sound of a drawer opening and closing, a beam of light lit up a wide swath across the floor. Her ghostlike reappearance took his breath away. “Do you know anyone who installs generators? The kind that kicks on automatically when the power goes out? A standby generator, I think it’s called. That’s the next upgrade I’m making to the building, even if it costs a bundle. I need more than emergency lighting and a temporary backup for the security system.”

“I’ll check with a few contractors I trust and let you know by the end of the week.” Glad for the distraction, he fished his cell from his pants pocket to add the task to his to-do list." You have access to a gas line, right?"

"Yes." With the light reflecting off the light-colored flooring, her blonde hair formed a halo around her head, the antithesis of the woman she imparted to the public eye. She looked nothing like the suspiciously too-convenient widow some people in town implied or outright accused her of being whenever she became the topic of gossip, especially since both men had been wealthy. As straightforward as she was, using poison to induce heart attacks didn't seem like her style at all. Hell, even a sex-induced aneurysm was far more believable than death by nightshade. "The temperature's going to drop pretty quickly if the power doesn't come back on soon, which isn't likely with this storm. Let's close the window and door shades to block out some of the cold. Then we can go in the office and shut the door since it's the smallest interior room. It should hold the heat longest. Plus, I have drinks, food, and comfortable furniture in there."

He gave a curt nod, glad her practicality tempered his unexpected reaction to her. "Good plan."

Her brisk pace to the front of the store challenged him to keep up, despite her short but shapely legs. She lowered the blinds closest to the checkout counter, blocking out the snowy scene before he reached the other window facing the parking lot. "Do you need to call anybody to let them know you're safe? There probably isn't much cell signal in this weather, but I have a landline for the shop."

Focusing on the job at hand instead of the potential chance to have a date, he shook his head. "Normally, I'd say yes, but my son's on a senior class trip this week. My daughter's in college and won't be home for spring break until Friday."

"No wife? Or significant other?"

Although the question sounded innocent enough, he couldn't help but wonder if she was fishing for information. "Nope. Divorced. No girlfriend."

The blinds on the entrance snapped at the bottom of the glass as Cerise seemed to look him up and down. After locking both deadbolts on the door, she grabbed a package of batteries and a box from one of the displays on her way back through the shop. "Hurry up. And before you ask, I got the condoms just in case. Hard to say how long the power will be out. I get bored easily."

He followed the wedge of light into the stockroom and toward her office, unsure whether he should be thrilled by the possibility of real sex for the first time in years or scared because of her casual mention of it. No way in hell would he be able to resist her invitation. The heavy *thunk* of the door closing behind him rang through the space like a hammer hitting the final nail in a coffin.

I'm fucked.

Well, not yet, but probably at some point.

She placed the batteries and the box of condoms on the coffee table—in plain sight until such time as she decided to turn off the flashlight—and gestured for him to sit on the couch. An unexpected smile curved her pink lips upward. "You should see your expression. Don't worry. I'm not going to jump your boner without your permission. Yes, I notice those things about men, especially since they can't exactly hide it. We may as well get comfortable."

Heat crawled across his face, assuring him he'd blushed. "I didn't mean to think about you in that way."

Her smile morphed into a wicked grin. "Why not? I'm thinking about you in *that way*. I'm single. You're single. We can have sex with each other if we want to, and I would never feel guilty for bringing myself or someone else pleasure. Have a seat. I promise not to bite. Nibbling is another story."

He dropped into the chair, not trusting her to keep her hands, mouth, and other body parts to herself any more than he could. "I don't sleep with every woman I meet."

"I don't sleep with every man I meet. Maybe I just want to make lubricated balloon animals." She winked at him a moment before she perched on the table facing him, her legs between his knees, and clicked off the flashlight.

Get *Hang-Ups*!

ABOUT THE AUTHOR

Mellanie Szereto is the *USA Today* Bestselling Author of over sixty romcoms and contemporary romances, most with characters who have plenty of life experience like herself. Whether you call them older, seasoned, mature, experienced, or later-in-life protagonists, they deserve love too! Her stories are often set in small towns with quirky main characters, fun secondary casts, and lots of humor. She enjoys gardening, cooking, and baking—as well as hiking to work off the fruits of her labor—and incorporates food into all of her stories. She lives in an old farmhouse in rural Indiana with her husband of thirty-eight years.

Visit her website for more information about her books!

www.ingramcontent.com/pod-product-compliance
Lightning Source LLC
LaVergne TN
LVHW020047110826
845155LV00029B/667

9781942522942